Edward Gilliat

Asylum Christi - A Story of the Dragonnades

Vol. I

Edward Gilliat

Asylum Christi - A Story of the Dragonnades
Vol. I

ISBN/EAN: 9783337274405

Printed in Europe, USA, Canada, Australia, Japan

Cover: Foto ©Andreas Hilbeck / pixelio.de

More available books at **www.hansebooks.com**

ASYLUM CHRISTI:

A STORY OF

THE DRAGONNADES.

By EDWARD GILLIAT, M.A.

IN THREE VOLUMES.
VOL. I.

LONDON:
SAMPSON LOW, MARSTON, SEARLE & RIVINGTON,
CROWN BUILDINGS, 188, FLEET STREET.
1877.

PREFACE.

THE reader will ask, "Is this true? Did it really happen?" To this must be replied that the De Cornelli family are creations of the author, but their fortunes and sufferings are historical, inasmuch as they happened, not once to one particular family, but over and over again to many persons, and in many parts of France.

The historical student will recognize old friends in Huet, Jean la Bruyère, the Abbess of Fontevraud, Du Chayla, Cavalier, and the other chiefs of the Huguenots in the Cevennes.

One liberty has been taken with chronology which must be acknowledged. In order to bring into contrast the Protestantism of the educated Normans with that of the unguided men of the desert, the rising in Languedoc has been represented as taking place in 1687, whereas the facts related did not occur until 1702.

The incidents related in that part of the story which deals with the Cevennes are taken impartially from Roman Catholic or Protestant historians ; but it has not been thought necessary to adhere strictly to the order of time in which those events took place.

All descriptions of scenery throughout the book have been suggested by personal inspection of the localities described.

E. G.

ASYLUM CHRISTI.

CHAPTER I.

IT is the spring of the year 1683 : the gardens which slope down, terrace after terrace, to those dark woods on which the westering sun will soon set are the domain of the Sieur de Cornelli, nobleman and landed proprietor in Normandy. The spires of yon cathedral to the east are the spires of the cathedral church of Coutances, and that bit of light beyond the woods far away to the west is the sea. The château itself is concealed from us by a cluster of cedars, as we stand on the upper terrace of the gardens ; but on this clear afternoon in May one can look over the rolling fields of fair Normandy till the eye can descry, faintly blurred in the golden sunset, the isle of Jersey ;

while, if we turn ourselves to the east, we can make out the rounded eminence of the little town of St. Lô, twenty-one miles away.

There is a rustic seat on a little knoll at the end of this terrace, which commands an extensive view on all sides, and half-a-dozen well-grown trees form a grateful canopy or shelter from the rain. It is to this secluded spot that two figures are making their way along the terrace—one, that of a tall and well-proportioned gentleman of about forty years, the other, that of a slim girl of eighteen. It is the sieur himself who comes towards us, bearing his *chapeau* under his arm—for this is the age of flowing wigs—and attired in a simple suit of black, and he is pointing out to the girl by his side the varying beauties of the landscape.

"I am charmed, mademoiselle, to think that you already find la belle Normandie so pleasing."

"Pleasing! Oh, monsieur! such scenery as this deserves a far more enthusiastic expression. I have never seen so extensive a prospect, even in dear old England!" A sigh, half-audible, half-suppressed, accompanied this allusion to her native country; her companion noticed it, and in a low, kind voice, replied—

"You speak, mademoiselle, of 'dear old England,' as if that land were endeared to you by a thousand associations of home and kindred; and yet my friend the English wine-merchant at Havre gave me to understand that you were an orphan, and had never known the sympathy of near kinsmen. Forgive me, Mademoiselle Ethel, if I seem to you to touch thus early on personal topics, but I do so— I recall to your mind these misfortunes—that I may assure you all the more warmly of our wish to make you one of us—to get you to feel that it was as my daughter's friend I brought you to live with us; long has she needed a sister, and in you, mademoiselle, I already feel she has found one."

Ethel Digby bowed in answer to these kindly meant but somewhat stately utterances; in truth, she was a little frightened by her patron's formal manner, and as this was only her first day at the Château de l'Esprit, and her fourth on French soil, she felt herself at present as amongst strangers.

Her parents had both died when she was almost an infant, and a maiden aunt had brought her up and given her a good education in Latin and English; for the example of

Queen Elizabeth had given a great stimulus to the education of women at this period, and the works of Spenser and Sidney, Shakspeare and Bacon, were read with avidity in an age whose taste had not been cloyed by the honeyed pages of the modern novelist.

Her aunt lived in a small house near Winchelsea, in Sussex, and this was the occasion of her gaining a knowledge of French—an unusual accomplishment for English men or women in that age; for there happened to be a colony of French refugees settled at Rye, which town lies within an easy walk of Winchelsea, and thus the liberal-minded aunt was enabled to give her niece the opportunity of learning to speak French with an accent racy of the soil, if not Parisian.

But the good old lady's affairs became embarrassed, and with her decaying income came the anxiety that sapped her health, and Ethel Digby found herself, at the age of seventeen, alone in the world and almost penniless. However, by the kindness of a merchant at Rye she was lodged and fed at little or no expense, until a wine-merchant from Havre, coming one day into the port, and inquiring for a young lady of parts and education to be companion to the daughter of a French nobleman, Ethel was consulted on the matter, and with a heavy heart agreed to accept the position.

After being buffeted about for several days between Rye and Havre on a stormy sea, it was with a sigh of relief that she stepped from the odorous cabin of the clumsy schooner upon the shore of a new and strange country.

That night she was lodged at the house of Master John Walters, the wine-merchant, and received gratefully the *petits soins* of madame, his little French wife, who spoke at great length on her capacity for making " English comforts," while all the time the arrangements of the house, the preparation of the food, and the painful primness of the furniture, bespoke her inability to understand the inner meaning of our insular word.

Ethel was, however, thankful for all mercies, and glad to sleep in a bed that did not turn somersaults during the night—her recent experience—and when early the next morning, a weather-beaten old coachman of the Sieur de Cornelli drove to the door with a covered carriage on springs, and a pair of what Ethel called "ponies" (to good old Pierre's disgust), she began to feel her spirits revive, and the adventure and the novelty of the journey kept her thoughts away from sad memories of the past.

It was, however, a long and tedious journey, and the roads were often so bad that Ethel was glad to descend and walk for a mile or two in the worst places ; and then Pierre, holding the near side pony by the bit with a terrific grip, as if the worst might be expected from such bone and mettle, would enter into conversation with the young *Anglaise*, and try to beguile the weary way with local tales and shrewd sayings.

Fortunately, Ethel had been accustomed to horses, and had often ridden out with a rich young lady of her acquaintance at Rye, and this experience had served her as a passport to Pierre's good graces. For towards the close of the second day's journey, as they were descending a steep hill, a part of the harness gave way, as French harness will do, and the carriage was running on to the hocks of the ponies, who were eyeing matters ascant in a fashion that exhibited a good deal of the white of the eye, when Ethel quietly jumped down from behind and pushed a thick stick between the spokes of the wheel— this was the drag in those parts of France—and before Pierre had time to get down, she had re-

arranged the straps and made the harness secure.
From this moment Pierre's feelings towards his
young *protégée* underwent a change—from the
helpless English mademoiselle, who might, for
all he knew, be a Papist, she was transformed
into a clever · and obliging companion ; and
Pierre soon began to open his heart to her
respecting the family in which she was going to
live, and the state of France in general ; and as
the conversation which enlightened Ethel may
also make the reader comprehend the position
of some of the characters that follow, we shall
take the liberty of listening to the travellers as
they journey.

It was after stopping a night at Caen, when
they were leaving the towers of St. Etienne in
the distance. There had been rain all night, and
at seven o'clock, when they partook of boiled
milk and hot bread, the sky was still dispensing
its superfluous drops, so that for the first mile
and a half neither spoke. But the clouds
cleared away and the sun shone out, making
all the dew-drops silver on the new spring
leaves, and the peasant-women, as they passed
on their way to the market, threw back their
dark hoods and smiled good-morning beneath
the bravery of their tall Norman caps. Old

Pierre relaxed his usual stern look, the ponies shook their heads merrily, and the little bells with which they were adorned rang out and jangled with unwonted energy.

"And perhaps mademoiselle finds Caen magnificent?" inquired Pierre, .pointing back with his whip in the direction of the gilded spires.

"I admired some of the churches, Pierre, very much, and the shops are well bestowed in jewellery, to my thinking."

"Humph! Churches and jewellery! Voyez-vous, mademoiselle, you have put your finger on the two curses of the town."

Ethel bit her lip and smiled; the old man whipped the ponies smartly, and, to compensate matters, pulled them in abruptly.

"I say to myself, mademoiselle is English; she is learned in the Scriptures, and, like her countrymen, is of 'the religion.'"

"'The religion?'" asked Ethel; "we are Protestants in England."

"Ah, well! mademoiselle can call it what she will—here we call it 'the religion.' Doubtless the English Protestants have some tincture of Papistry amongst them still, for I observed that mademoiselle avoided the temple service last night, and seemed to be captivated by the false glitter of the altars."

" Indeed, if you call that bare chamber in which I saw a Calvinist preaching in a black gown 'the temple,' I must confess to feeling a shiver run through me when he shouted out that description of the bottomless pit. Besides, Pierre, it was not a bit like a church, and clergy and laity seemed all dressed alike."

" Mon Dieu! to hear mademoiselle speak, one would fancy she came from the court of the Grand Monarque! I could take mademoiselle to our temple in Coutances, where she would hear such a description of hell-fire as would send her weeping to bed, and glad enough to get there safely! But, after all, doubtless mademoiselle is of the elect, and so it makes no matter." Whereupon Pierre scolded the off-side pony for an imaginary stumble, and resumed, in a quieter tone, " In effect, it is no easy matter for us at the château to live up to our religious lights without offending the Catholic scruples and superstitions of madame."

" What! Is Madame de Cornelli, then, a Catholic ? "

" To be sure she is. Does not mademoiselle know that the Sieur de Cornelli fell in love with a lady at the king's court, and that the queen was very angry with her for marrying a Calvinist—though, for the matter of that, my master was then, they say, more of an infidel than aught else, and used to mock at our doctrines of election and justification. But since times have been changing for the worse, and 'the religion' has been hampered and restricted by laws and ordinances, and the king has been trying to bribe the elect of God to take the mass and go to confession, the sieur has been more regular in his attendance at divine worship; I will say that for him."

"You surprise me, my good Pierre; I quite thought I was going amongst Protestants. And, pray what is the young lady?"

"Oh, Mademoiselle Marie is Catholic, like her mamma; it was arranged that the sons should follow the father's religion, and the daughters the mother's. Voilà!"

Whether this last expression was intended to give point to his explanation, or whether it was the outward symbol of the gratification he felt in having successfully touched up the off-side pony on a raw place, I don't know; but as the whip thereby became entangled in the harness, it was incumbent on Pierre to dismount, and

Ethel found, upon his climbing to his seat, that
the old man had for some unaccountable reason
contracted an obstinate tendency to silence. So
she left him to his gutturals and his ponies, and
commenced building castles in the air, with the
hope of charming away a certain instinctive
feeling of dread which Pierre's account of the
Château de l'Esprit had given her. In vain!
She found herself thinking over the thrilling
incidents of the Bartholomew Massacre, dwelling
morbidly on scenes from the siege of Rochelle,
which an old sea-captain had related to her, and
drawing vivid pictures of thumb-screws and
scavenger's-daughters, until, tired and worn, she
sank into a deep slumber which even the jolt-
ing of the vehicle could not disturb; and thus
she rested until a vague sense of stopping and
of confused voices made her start up, and—
could she believe her eyes?—there, in the slant
rays of the afternoon sun, sat on her white palfry
a young girl, with long braided hair falling in two
brown tresses down her back. The dark gray
eyes, fringed with long black lashes, and crowned
with eyebrows whose curving lines gave a very
arch and piquant look to the face, the blue
riding-dress fitting close to the girlish figure,
the long black plume that rose beside the

steeple hat and drooped backward—all flashed
at once upon Ethel's bewildered gaze, and
she could find no words for utterance. The
other, however, advancing to the side of the
carriage, leaned forward and stretched out a
hand of welcome, adding, in a bright and cheer-
ful tone—

"We bid you welcome, Mademoiselle Digby,
to Normandy. I must introduce myself—I am
Marie de Cornelli, and this little boy is my
brother Philippe. We have ridden so far to
meet you, and to escort you to the house of our
aunt, who will give us shelter for the night, and
to-morrow we shall finish the journey very
easily."

Ethel said some words of questionable French
in answer to her companion, which were not
improved by an English translation that a
natural confusion of mind prompted her to
supply, as Marie knew no English ; but the
mistake at once dismounted them from the stilts
of ceremony, and in a few minutes they were
laughing together like old friends.

Marie now gave her palfry to a groom to
lead, and took a place in the carriage beside
Ethel. Pierre gave an extra crack to his whip
and the cavalcade proceeded. Behind the car-

riage rode the little Philippe, a blue-eyed boy of twelve years, clad in a doublet of purple satin, over which passed a shoulder-belt of silk cord, to which was attached a small hunting-horn ; in his hat was a black aigrette ; his feet were encased in large leather stirrups, and he carried a silver-mounted whip with a long lash. It was not at first sight quite clear what was the use of the horn and dog-whip, but in answer to Philippe's call a large tawny mastiff jumped out of the gorse by the wayside.

" Maintenon " was a young dog, scarcely a year old, but already gave promise of considerable power ; however, he seemed to think that his young master was a younger dog than he, and, perhaps in consequence of too often reiterated commands, philosophically turned a deaf ear, and pursued his sanitary inspections on either side of the road, in scorn of consequences.

Nothing remarkable occurred that evening. It was getting dusk as they rode into the grounds of the Sieur de Cornelli's sister. She received them with open arms, and entertained them with fish from the lake and sweet-meats of her own concocting, kissed them all on both cheeks when they went to bed, and called them early the next morning to pray for a blessing on the day about to come. This was Ethel's introduction to a Calvinist household, and she was a little frozen by the stern and severe looks of the worshippers, as they stood and repeated the fifty-first Psalm.

But however uncompromising the good old lady showed herself to her Creator, to flesh and blood she was the most winning of maiden aunts; and thus the harsh features of her religion did not make so deep an impression on Ethel's mind. They left her waving a kerchief wet with tears, and repeating aloud a verse of the Psalm they had read in the morning.

"Aunt Justine is a good, kind creature," said Marie, as they drove away, "but she always makes me attend her heretical services, in the hope, I presume, that I may join the religion."

"Does Madame de Cornelli object to your attending a Protestant service? I think Pierre told me she and you were Catholics," said Ethel.

"Certainly, mamma would not wish me to do so, except out of politeness to my friends; one must be civil, you know, and unfortunately our family is afflicted with many heretics. Mamma, to be sure, is a good Catholic—you should hear the Bishop of Coutances sing her praises; as for me, I have not thought much about such things."

"But your little brother there—is he the same as your papa?"

" Oh! the Cornelli family have been Huguenots for a century and more—it is a point of honour with papa, more than of religion, I think; but men, you understand, do not make good Catholics—they seem to me to lack that feeling of dependence which makes a woman so willing to submit to the penance of Holy Church.   Why, that little villain, Phil, is a rank Huguenot!   He and Pierre shut themselves up in the stable and sing Marot's hymns.   It is scandalous!"

They were now approaching the little town of St. Lô, and as the carriage moved slowly up the steep hill on which the town stands, the white-capped peasants thronged about them on all sides—for it was market-day—and some of them dropped a reverence to Marie, which she acknowledged with a smile and a nod.   It was to Ethel a novel sight, accustomed as she had been to a peasantry not over nice and elegant in their attire; and the perfect neatness and cleanliness of these poor women, with their pats of butter in a white linen cloth, surprised and amused her. She was still more astonished when she noticed that the first thing each woman did on attaining the summit of the hill was to enter the church which stood at the further end of the market-place. At Ethel's request the party stopped at the church door; and upon their entering, a large number of men and women of the poorer classes were found kneeling before the various altars, absorbed in their devotions.

"Is it not a beautiful idea, the unity of worshippers—a whole nation knit together in one common house of God!" whispered Marie.

Ethel thought of the scenes of drunkenness which disgraced her own country, and assented.

Presently they came out, but not before Marie had reverently knelt on the cold stones before the high altar. As they approached the carriage, they saw that a crowd of market-people had collected, and angry voices were awakening echoes in the sacred precincts. The centre of the surging crowd, Philippe and Pierre, were being held at bay, and Maintenon was struggling savagely in the leash. The ponies, left to themselves, were browsing on the green weed that grew beside the church.

"Ma foi! what shall we do? they will hurt poor little Phil!"

Ethel sprang forward, forced her way through the press, and in a moment was standing beside Philippe. The sudden appearance of a girl who was at least a head taller than any woman there startled the crowd into silence. Her long fair hair had fallen from its moorings and had drifted rippling to her waist; her face, usually pale, was crimsoned with emotion.; and, raising one hand, she bade them respect the sanctity of the place, and depart in peace.

The peasants looked a little ashamed, but soon a score of voices began to murmur, "Why, then, did they sing their cursed hymns at the door of our church?" and the tumult grew louder.

Ethel then, for the first time, began to feel afraid. It was as if the reason of the individual was being swallowed up by the animal nature of the species; the fierce, glowing eyes came nearer and nearer, and the cursing of the women made her blood curdle. As for poor Marie, she stood on the church steps, weeping and wringing her hands. Philippe would have struck at the crowd with his riding-whip, but Ethel prevented him; Maintenon was snarling

and showing very white teeth, and Pierre was
disposing himself as much like the old picture
of the Christian martyr in his saddle-room at
the château as he conveniently could.

The situation was becoming worse and worse,
when the roll of a drum caught Marie's ear, and
she instantly ran off in quest of help. A company of marines in their blue jackets were
escorting some stores from St. Malo, and had
just halted on the green at the back of the
church : a young officer was with them. Marie
rushed up to him, and breathlessly begged his
help to save her friends from the mob who
surrounded them. She had not lifted her eyes
to the young officer's face, and she started when
he said, " Marie ! You here, and want my
protection !" Then, turning to his men, he gave
the word of command to fall in, and, drawing
his sabre, marched at their head into the narrow
street where the crowd were pushing and yelling.
In a moment a cry was raised, "*Les militaires!*"
and, right and left, men in blouses and white-
capped women gave way or fled, and left the
marines masters of the field.

All was order and quiet in a few minutes,
and when Marie had again approached the
church, she found Lieutenant Guillot and

Philippe shaking each other by the hand and exchanging salutes on either cheek. The marines stood fast at "attention," and only a faint smile on some faces betrayed a passing interest in what was going forward. After Marie had expressed her thanks to Lieutenant Henri, as she called him, for his prompt assistance, the two ladies were escorted to the carriage, and old Pierre, looking rather crestfallen, gathered up the reins.

"I am so much obliged to you, Henri," said Marie, as she leaned forward to shake the lieutenant by the hand, while a blush deepened the colour of her cheek and neck.

"And I am so much obliged to the *canaille* there," said Henri, bowing; "but for them I might never have seen my friend, and——"

Guillot seemed at a loss for a word and stammered confusedly. Marie, too, was confused, and cried out, "Drive on, Pierre;" and amongst the cracking of whips and the jangling of bells Marie caught the words, "Adieu, mademoiselle, until the day of your *fête.*"

There was a silence between the two girls for some minutes; it was broken at last by Ethel exclaiming, "How very foolish of Pierre to sing his hymns close to the church!"

"Yes, indeed! and quite contrary to law—but that is the way with these Huguenots; they are as obstinate as a Breton."

"It was lucky, your meeting with a friend in the lieutenant."

"Oh! Henri Guillot used to live at Coutances when he was a little boy. His mother had a house on my father's estate; there she and her three sons used to remain while the father, le capitaine, was away on service at sea. They are all in the navy, those Guillots. The father is an old friend of our family."

"What beautiful dark eyes, and what a strong handsome man!"

"Ah! you find him handsome enough, then? But did you not see the sweet little dimple that nestled in his cheek when he smiled? Did you not mark it, mademoiselle?"

"I did, truly, and also the row of strong white teeth, and the clear, almost girl-like, complexion. But for his blue uniform I should have taken him for an Englishman; he had a very open, ingenuous look."

"Thank you for an equivocal compliment," said Marie, laughing; "we Normans, then, are not usually ingenuous!"

"I beg pardon—it is our English conceit to fancy ourselves so."

"The Guillot family, however, are Breton, I have heard papa say; they are not, indeed, noble by birth."

"Are there many noble families in this neighbourhood, mademoiselle?"

"Not so many as there were a few years ago. When the great Colbert came into power he revoked all titles to nobility under thirty years' standing, so many of the *nouveaux riches* had claimed a title."

"And do the nobility in France marry with the middle class?" said Ethel, with an arch look at her companion.

"It depends!" answered Marie, with a haughty toss of the head; "some of the old nobility are very select."

They were now approaching the little town of Coutances. The cathedral rose before them on the summit of the hill they were climbing: its gray towers rose heavenward through no vile cloud of smoke; unsullied and unsoiled, that house of God seemed a fit emblem of the religious life it was reared to enkindle—its foundations were fixed amongst the homes of men, its old gray buttresses and lantern spires pointed to the blue heights beyond.

As the carriage rattled over the pavement in

the narrow streets, it seemed as though a city
had risen to life again—doors were flung open,
and old beldames in close-fitting caps peered out
to see what was the cause of all the clatter.   It
was noon, and Coutances was clearly taking a
late *déjeûner*. Stalwart young men, who, Ethel
thought, ought to have been at work, came forth
to view the travellers, holding most of them a
dish of *bouillon*, or vegetable broth, in the left
hand. The booths of the merchants and trades-
people were at this hour deserted, or left in the
fearful charge of a young girl, allowing barely
space enough for the carriage to pass. Should
they have been so unfortunate as to meet
another vehicle, one of the two would have
been compelled to back into a side street, when
there would have been no lack of officious
hands to turn the wheels or hold the horses.
However, our travellers safely passed the
dangers of the streets, and were soon climbing
a hill to the west of the town. There was
wood now on either hand, more like the woods of
Sussex which Ethel had missed so much in her
drive through Normandy, where the oak raised
his giant arms and the elm flung about him
his stately foliage.

They had driven a little more than two miles

from Coutances when they arrived at a massive stone gateway on the right hand side of the road. Over the top of the arch which spanned the drive ran a device in Latin: "Non si malè nunc, et olim sic erit," and grinning in cold gray stone above that rose a lion with an ambitious tail and an iron chain about his neck. The benighted peasant's teeth had often chattered when the gray lion clanked his chain at midnight—for so the legend ran. At one side of the gateway there was a door in the stone-work, and from this issued an old woman with a face like a Ribston-pippin, who hobbled to the gate and slowly unfastened the ponderous bolts. As Ethel gazed at the wizened face of the old hag she felt she must have seen its counterpart, and her wonder was allayed when she saw Pierre stoop down and smack the pippin on both cheeks, with a "Good-day, mother." As they passed through the gate, Marie nodded to the old mother, who in return made a slow and stately curtsey.

The drive led them through a portion of the wood into a cleared space where trees of rare beauty seemed to be performing solos to the distant but admiring thickets ; presently smoke appeared curling over the tree-tops—blue wood

smoke, which gave a tone to the sylvan picture
—and, turning suddenly round a clump of
cedars, the travellers found themselves drawn
up beneath a long portico supported on stone
pillars. It was the Château de l'Esprit, and in
a moment the Sieur de Cornelli was at the door
to welcome them, with three or four servants in
livery behind him.

Ethel had only time to notice a fine, handsome, rather dark face, with iron-grey eyes and
black moustachios, when the sieur advanced,
and, kissing her hand, assisted her into the hall.
As she passed to the 'further end her eye fell
upon the suits of armour which hung by the
wall, some battered and dusty, others bright
and seeming but of yesterday ; at the further
end a fire was blazing, and plates were disposed
on either side to catch the heat. In the centre
was a table, spread with a clean white cloth,
where the higher servants were about to eat
their dinner. After warming themselves for
a few minutes at the fire, the sieur led the way
to an inner chamber where food was being
served for the travellers, and when he had seen
that all was fitly provided, he made his excuses
and left the two girls alone with Philippe.

Madame de Cornelli was not very well, and

was in her own room; so after dinner the young ladies retired to their separate apartments, and when, late in the afternoon, Ethel came into the hall, she found the sieur about to stroll in the garden, and, joining him, had the conversation recorded in the early part of this chapter.

CHAPTER II.

It was the evening of the third day after
Ethel's arrival at the château. Madame de
Cornelli was reclining on a couch in her red
boudoir; the log was making fireworks up the
wide chimney, and pouring a stream of red light
upon the closed curtains · and damask chairs.
An elegant confusion seemed to prevail in the
chamber—a guitar lay upon the table, a mass-
book lay upon the guitar, some leaves of music
were shed upon the floor like autumnal waifs,
and an oaken *prie-Dieu* supported a volume of
plays by the king's *valet-de-chambre*, as he was
commonly styled—the famous Molière. A pair
of gauntlets trimmed with marten's fur lay
beside the couch, and almost touching the
gloves, but more in the shadow and under the
sofa, you might have seen a black muzzle and a
pair of bright, watchful eyes. Maintenon would

not have let you touch a treasure he was ordered to protect.

But let us turn to the lady who lies looking dreamily on the flying sparks.

Madame de Cornelli was married eighteen years ago, or a little more; she was now thirty-seven years old. She had been a great favourite with the queen, to whom she had lent her services as maid-of-honour, and by her she had been imbued with strong religious feelings, which, if they did not take the place of natural levity and coquetry, at least struggled hard for a prominent position in her list of virtues. She had, however, more wit than her mistress, the good-natured Maria Theresa, and contrived to win the affections of a young Norman nobleman who had come up to Paris with a Huguenot deputation.

The Sieur de Cornelli was five years her senior—at that time a tall, handsome young man of twenty-three, with an unencumbered estate; known in literary circles as a philosopher and savant, the friend of Malebranche, Bayle, and Racine—but then he was a Huguenot! The queen would not listen to such an idea as her maid-of-honour marrying a heretic. But clever men were just then in fashion, and

Mademoiselle de Laselle, as she never missed
going to confession, so she never failed to follow
the turns and windings of Dame Fashion;
besides, she was then but eighteen years old,
and it was quite *à la mode* to fall in love at
an age so tender.   Accordingly she fled one
morning in a coach and four, was privately
married in Paris, and before the ladies of the
court had time to whisper a word of scandal,
Madame de Cornelli was half-way on her road
to her husband's château in Normandy.   Her
soft blue eyes and fair hair, her sweet liquid
voice, her winning helplessness and air of listless discontent, at first took the love of the sieur
by storm ; he hovered about her as the moth
does about the candle, and singed the wings of
his intellect in the process.   But time opened
his eyes to defects which he was once content
to worship, and the image of beauty which at
first monopolized the shrine of his affections
began, as years went by and children came to
claim his care, to occupy a niche in a humbler
corner, a little battered, yet not unnoticed.

No ! Madame, under her listless and *distrait*
manners, possessed a shrewd and practical sense,
the use of which kept her ever in her husband's
esteem, when her personal charms alone might

have had but a temporary conquest. The sieur had never tried to make a convert of her to Calvinism, believing that for most women the leading strings of Catholicism were safer than the perilous liberty of religious revolution. And so madame had her private chapel and her confessor in one part of the château, while her husband and his Huguenot followers praised God in the other.

She had arrived at the age when ladies, beginning to miss the old absorbing charm of being daily flattered by those they love, turn, as a kind of *dernier ressort*, to the consolations of their favourite chaplains, and when, from hearing themselves praised for earthly accomplishments, which they owe solely to the bounty of Nature, they turn with a sigh of half-pleased resignation to the affectionate reproof of their confessor, when he chides them in fair, soft words for spiritual defects which none but he has been privileged to detect.

And yet we must do madame the justice to say that she was, or believed herself to be, thoroughly in earnest when she forsook the *rôle* of a woman of fashion and gave herself to frequent fasts and secret penance. And her religion, cumbered though it was with priestly finger-posts and ecclesiastical half-way houses, was a road which was bringing her daily nearer God. She grew more unselfish—the one true test of growth in holiness—and her unselfishness was not bounded by the limits of her family; she did not flatter her soul that God and the Church approved her if she was lavish to those she loved and spent herself in the service of her children. By the advice of Monseigneur the Bishop of Coutances, whose fine, dark face and lustrous eyes seemed to her as the vision of an angel, she had vowed to devote no small portion of her time to visiting the sick and the poor in and about the town of Coutances; and the work, which she had commenced with some repugnance, and from a desire to achieve some holy work whereby she might be saved, had somehow done more for her in this life than she had expected. New and larger sympathies began to ennoble a foolish life. She awoke to the fact that in the reeking cabin of the meanest peasant joy and sorrow, light and shadow, pleasure and pain, were felt as keenly as in the gilded palace, and she had seen how Christ and our Blessed Lady did not scorn to make their home amongst the scum and outcast of the land. She had deemed that her works ot mercy and charity were to be set on one side, like so many leaves out of a ledger, to vouch for her future salvation ; she little understood how those very works were working out her soul's salvation—even in their doing—in the higher purpose which they suggested to her energies, in the learning of her Lord's sweet lessons of humility and self-surrender. It was not the *result* of all her labours that was to save her, but the *process* itself—the uncomplaining, the waiting, the long toiling in dark streets, the kneeling beside fevered couches, and on the cold altar-steps when the wax lights flickered in the wintry gust. In doing such-like things she was not earning an eternal reward, nick-named "Salvation," to be paid her on demand after funeral obsequies ; no ! her soul was being saved alive, as the old writing hath it, here in this world and for the next.

As she lay there reclining on the sofa after the labours of a day spent in attending mass at the cathedral and visiting a few poor *protégées*, Madame de Cornelli was revolving in her mind certain projects regarding the future welfare of her daughter, the wilful, too-natural Marie. For we must not suppose that the Church occupied all her thoughts ; she was too good a

Catholic not to put the Church first, at least in fancy, but she was too good a mother not to sacrifice a little principle for her children's benefit. The scheme which she was proposing to herself just now was an alliance between Marie and the Comte de Pontorson, a young nobleman of wealth and influence in the neighbourhood, a Catholic, but of unenviable fame for his lax and extravagant mode of living.

"But then," said madame to herself, casting her eyes to the gilded ceiling, "it will be Marie's *rôle* to win that young man's soul for Christ and His Holy Church." Marie would be seventeen in a few days' time, and great preparations were being made at the château to render her *fête* as elegant as possible. All the gentry for many miles around had accepted invitations to a grand ball to be given in honour of Marie's birthday, and many families were coming to spend the day and take part in the religious ceremonies which usually formed part of the day's proceedings. Madame de Cornelli had therefore much to think about, besides mass-books and wax-candles.

It was while she was engaged in a reverie so pleasing to ladies, in which a certain handsome young bridegroom leads from the altar a certain blushing young bride—when a sympathetic smile was breaking over her face and recalling the charms of eighteen years ago—that a sudden angry bark from Maintenon made her start from the sofa and peer into the shadows of the boudoir. At the same time a voice cried—

"A thousand pardons, madame, if I disturb you; will you have the kindness to restrain your dog, that I may enter the chamber?"

"Down, Maintenon, down, I tell you!" cried madame. The dog came from under the sofa, looked up inquiringly into the face of his mistress, then sat on his haunches facing the stranger, who entered the room, bowing low. By the glimmer of the fire, as he bowed his head, you might have seen that the dark, short-cut hair which covered his head bore marks of the tonsure, though not of very recent cutting; the long serge habit, confined at the waist by a cord, the tassels of which fell almost to the knee, concealed a figure which was, though spare, lithe and active. The new-comer was one of those who write S.J. after their name; he was a priest of the famous Society of Jesus, and was newly arrived from Paris on affairs touching the diocese of Coutances. Having met

Madame de Cornelli at the bishop's residence,
he had contrived to procure an invitation to
stay a few days at the château, where he assisted Father Beauvais, madame's private chap-
lain, in those little ecclesiastical attentions which
were customary in the sieur's household.

"Ah! come in, your reverence—it is Father
Beretti, is it not?"

There was soon no doubt of the father's
identity, for, as he moved to take the seat to
which his hostess motioned him, a shining silver
crucifix disengaged itself from the folds of his
habit, and swung pendulous from his neck as
he leaned forward to express a few words of
friendly interest in the occupations of the day.
Madame de Cornelli half-raised herself upon
her elbow, and the colour came to her cheek as
she conversed with the handsome young Jesuit.
There was something wanting, however, in
the striking face of the priest which made you
reserve your admiration, and you could not
help searching in those fine, glittering black
eyes for some traces of softness. There was a
hardness, too, about the thin lips which gave an
unpleasant expression to the face when it was
not lit up by smiles; and though every attitude
and gesture of this refined and cultured scholar

was subdued to a tone of deep humility, he
could not help letting you see the native pride
which underlay his professional and acquired
submission.   Perhaps it was because he showed
such *fierté*, and was so *point-device* in his ecclesiastical garb, that madame felt a fascination in
his voice and features which she experienced in
no other's, unless it were her bishop's.

"Here is a gentleman," she once remarked
to Marie, "and one who has mixed in all the
most learned and distinguished society of the
court; the friend of Père la Chaise and La
Fontaine—a priest as far above our country
fathers, as Abbé Huet is above his religious
confrères."

But Marie had taken a dislike to the Jesuit,
and her mother's praise of him fell on deaf ears.
There was another individual in the house who
also disliked the new guest, and that was Maintenon, a dog of strong Huguenot propensities,
insomuch as he had been once or twice soundly
beaten for venturing into the cathedral after
his mistress, whereas he had frequently followed
the sieur into the temple at Coutances, and
had slept out many a long dissertation on free-
will, at the feet of his master.   The mastiff had
accordingly chosen his side, and, with the ex-

ception of Father Beauvais, who lived at the château, he regarded all persons arrayed in priestly habits as suspicious characters.

The Jesuit had been conversing for some minutes with madame when the door opened and Marie entered; then, catching sight of the père, she curtsied and was about to retire, but Beretti rose, and softly bringing a *fauteuil* to her mother's side, begged her, with one of his most winning smiles, to seat herself.

" Yes, Marie, sit down and listen to what our good friend tells us of Paris and the fall of the Reformed."

" I was telling your noble mother, my daughter, of the great and good influence exercised upon his Majesty by that extraordinary woman, Madame de Maintenon "—the mastiff cocked one ear upon hearing his own name pronounced, and appeared to listen very gravely. " I was saying how, by God's interposition, this accomplished lady, once, as you know, the instructress of the royal children, had been enabled to turn a profligate heart to think of eternity and the condition of our Holy Church."

Marie answered drily, " Indeed! I thought Madame de Maintenon was a far different person ; we never speak of her here."

It was now the Jesuit's turn to colour ; he played a little sadly with the chain of his crucifix, and answered, in a serious tone—

"Pardon me, daughter, if I caution you against believing all the bad things you hear of illustrious people. Coutances is a long way from Paris—still, somehow, scandal travels faster and farther than good fame. Though the English play-writer tell us how 'shines a good deed in a naughty world,' yet, believe me, a breath of ill-report dims the glasses through which we most of us view our neighbours."

"I am glad to think I have been so unjust in my estimation," replied Marie, haughtily tossing her head.

"I used to think with you, daughter, that in the beautiful retreats of the country all was simplicity and truth and nature—that in the crowded city or the luxurious court there was more falsehood, duplicity, and wickedness. A few years of experience soon lead one to modify this hasty impression ; it is easy to mistake stagnation for simplicity, ill-nature for candour, and self-conceit for independence of character."

"I would rather stagnate amongst honest people and virtuous fools than live in yonder selfish court—and lose my self-respect."

"Well, daughter, I cannot but applaud your
sentiments, which breathe a spirit of local
patriotism which at least does honour to your
heart—and I am sure no one could accuse you
of intellectual stagnation or ill-nature. If I
might presume on my holy office so far as to
suggest a more submissive spirit—you will forgive me, I know—what are the laws of etiquette
when the soul is in danger? how can I help
feeling an interest in the eternal welfare of one
so young—and so thoughtless ?"

This appeal rendered Marie silent. The spell
was upon her; accustomed to listen to the
words of a priest as to the voice of God, she
could not hear Father Beretti's deep, solemn
tones accusing her of the sin of thoughtlessness
and pride without a feeling of shame and dismay; and when her mother drew her face to
her, and, kissing her on the forehead, whispered,
" Dearest Marie, think on what the good father
says, and pray our Lady to intercede for you,
and all will yet be well"—the poor girl was
quite overcome, and the tears trickled down her
cheeks.   They were tears of disappointment
rather than of remorse : she felt that this Jesuit
was putting her in a false light; that her mother,
who ought to have aided her and sided with her,

had failed to understand her; and she was very miserable.

As for the good father, he eyed the pearly tears with an inward chuckle; were they not the first-fruits of his disciplinary lecture? was he not breaking the head of what promised to be a rebellion against his priestly authority? and after a long pause, he resumed—

"Yes, as I was remarking before, good often comes from evil, or rather, what we in our ignorance deem evil; for what is good in one age becomes evil in the next, and *vice versâ*; and to speak of 'doing evil that good may come,' as our enemies of the Reformed Religion, so pretended, accuse us of the Society of Jesus, is utter nonsense. For, consider, my daughter, if it be really evil that we do, how can we conceive good springing from it? how can we believe that God will bless evil means? But, blessed be God and our Lady, good has resulted and does result from our labours; for instance, the king is even now working for the spread of the Catholic faith, the heresies of Jansenism and Quietism have come to naught, and Pelisson is daily making a fabulous number of conversions. Judge, then, if our means be not good which bring in so rich a harvest of blessed results!

No, my daughter! if good results from the means one employs—not accidentally, but as the direct result of those means—then those means are good—for good produces good, and evil evil. Shall we call God the Father of Lies? and Satan the Parent of Virtue? God forbid!"

The two ladies murmured their assent, the elder admiringly, the younger in a dazed and bewildered manner. The Jesuit continued—

"Madame de Maintenon is a lady of great and deep piety. Of her relations to the king, as they have not yet been made public, it is best to say but little; I will only tell you that they have received the sanction of the Church. And I am sure you will both agree with me in commending the zeal and judgment which that lady has shown in winning the heart of the king from the worldly career to which he has hitherto devoted himself. It only shows us how careful we should be what persons we choose for our friends, what influences may mould us for good or evil in the society of our nearest and dearest. Ah! my daughters, how I pray all the saints to keep you true amid the terrible temptations to which, in this country,— I might say, in this château especially,—you are exposed."

At this point the mastiff gave a whimper of impatient joy; was he, too, out-argued by the wily father? The foolish beast bounded across the room and put his nose to the bottom of the door, and with a firm and stately step entered the Sieur de Cornelli. Father Beretti rose in an instant and greeted his host with a frank and open smile—a smile, however, which after a time grew a little sickly and stereotyped, betraying the conscious effort to keep it. As these two men fronted one another, they betrayed no sense of antagonism; each seemed bent on showing the other with what courtesy he could disguise his real sentiments. De Cornelli was the taller of the two and by some years the senior. Beretti was about thirty-six years of age, but his smooth face and healthy glow made him look younger. De Cornelli was physically the stronger, but his student habits had made him stoop a little and had drawn the colour from his cheek. Beretti had exercised his intellect in action, in the disputations of the schools, in teaching at the Jesuit seminaries, and again in all the exciting and mixed society of the court of Louis the Fourteenth. De Cornelli was a reader of books; there was no one in the district with whom he could exchange ideas; his best thoughts had "passed into smother." He was a little indecisive, and apt to stammer and get confused in argument.

Beretti had an eye which seemed to pierce you through and through. De Cornelli, when he looked at you, seemed to be regarding something beyond you; often when he answered you he was thinking of something quite different. He was the deeper thinker of the two; Beretti was the quicker. You might have taken De Cornelli for a fool; Beretti would have impressed you with his ability in five minutes. De Cornelli was disguising his dislike to the father from the honourable feeling of courtesy towards a guest staying in his house; Beretti was disguising his animosity towards the Huguenot noble that good might come of it; he was smiling "in majorem Dei gloriam."

The conversation soon turned upon the approaching *fête*, and the quality and character of the guests invited. Amongst these were mentioned the names of Captain Guillot and Lieutenant Henri, the same who rescued our young ladies from the market-women of St. Lô.

"I have heard of that Guillot," said the Jesuit; "he is an old sea captain, I believe, whom his Majesty was compelled to supersede on account of his dangerous views, both religious and political. His son, too, if I mistake not, is also marked for retirement; they are a bad family."

De Cornelli smiled a little contemptuously, and replied, "The poor old man has done his duty gallantly for God and his country; he, at all events, has not been chary of his life to protect his Majesty, and when the grey hairs came, and his strength had been well-nigh spent in the service, an · ambitious woman finds him dangerous, and gets the king to fling him aside like a rotten apple. Poor old gentleman! he was staying with us when the order came for his dismissal, and I shall never forget the impression he made upon us by his heart-broken exclamations. Sir, if a man steel his heart with all the philosophy of the ancients, I defy him to crush the indignant thoughts that rise in his bosom when such deep ingratitude, such cruel injustice, is done an old officer. Sir, the family may be a bad family—the gentlemen of your society should be good judges of good and evil —but let me tell you, Father Beretti, that I know no man on this earth whose friendship I value more than that of old Captain Guillot, the Huguenot officer."

" Doubtless, monseigneur, the reports which came from his fellow-officers of his atheism and revolutionary principles were exaggerated ; but his Majesty, after well weighing the evidence, was reluctantly obliged to give way to the clamour which his unpopularity raised against him—and, as you say, he was already . past service."

" Excuse me," replied De Cornelli; " I said nothing of the sort. You people of the court are strangely misinformed on provincial matters, methinks; for it is a fact that nearly all the officers of the fleet deeply regretted Guillot's retirement—and, indeed, a petition was forwarded to the king that he might retain his commission. But is it true that the son, too, is ordered to retire ? "

" I saw him in command of a company of marines the other day, papa, and he said nothing to us about it."

" I may be premature," said the Jesuit, " but it was spoken of as probable ; and, indeed, the king no longer needs the services of Huguenots."

" May he never require them!" said De Cornelli with a sigh, and left the chamber.

Madame de Cornelli resumed, " I very much
regret that the Guillots were invited to attend
Marie's *fête*. Had I known as much of the old
officer's real sentiments as I do now, I should
have begged the sieur to pass them over."

"Oh, mamma! how can you say so! You
know it is because they are not Catholics that
Father Beretti objects to them. Is it not so,
father ? "

The Jesuit looked at Marie with a long
melancholy gaze, then sighed and moved his
lips as in prayer, and finally rose to leave the
room, bowing low to madame and her daughter,
only adding—

" Alas! for the evil that one human heart
may work upon another! Beware, daughter,
beware in time! The days are coming when our
faith will be tried to the uttermost—and woe to
that soul which deserts our Lord and His Holy
Church in the day of temptation. I go to pray
our Lady and all the saints for you and yours."

As the door closed upon the departing
father, Madame de Cornelli started from the
sofa with flashing eyes and a flushed face.

" Fie upon thee, Marie, for an irreverent

child, thus to anger the good father with thy impertinent speeches! Yes, he is right. He knows the heart of my poor child better than I do myself; it is the evil influence of Lieutenant Henri which makes thy proud spirit rebel against priestly authority.. I see it all now. Would to God I had never allowed him to cross our threshold! and he an ignoble adventurer, a person of no birth or ancestry!"

"There you do him wrong, my mother; his ancestors were ever famous amongst the officers of the navy."

"Oh, I grant you they were honest men and brave, but they are not noble."

Marie began to weep, and stammered out, pouting like a spoilt child—

"By your leave, my mother, they were noble, all are noble who do noble deeds—papa says so —they are noble in God's eyes, and a title is only a human recognition of nobility."

"O ciel! my child, what Republican sentiments! Go, get you to your chamber until supper-time—your eyes are red with weeping, and we expect guests to-night; go, dear child, get your rosary and say a prayer for humility; go, you will find rose-water in my pink-chamber. Such red eyes I never beheld."

And so Marie went away sobbing and rebellious, with fractious tear-drops resting on her
dark eye-lashes, which were too proud to fall
on the pretty, transparent cheek, and remained
like the last rain-drops on the rose when the
storm has passed away.

Then madame rose to change her travelling-
dress, and, preceded by a reverend old waiting-
woman, who carried a torch and a bundle of
keys, she ascended the wide oak staircase to
her private apartments.

Meanwhile great preparations were being
made in the left wing of the château, where the
servants' apartments and the kitchens were
situated, and cooks were running to and fro
with steaming dishes, while the footmen, in the
red livery of the sieur, lounged about by the
great fire in the servants'-hall, and discussed
their master and mistress. Of these old Pierre
was the most noisy, his red, weather-beaten face
looking redder by the glare of the sputtering
logs, and taking a deeper colour from the
potency of the cider, a jug of which he was
holding in his right hand. He was talking to
an old grey-headed man who stood the centre
of a listening group ; the shoulder-knots on his
livery were fuller and more elaborate than those

of the other servants, and he was inclining his head to listen to Pierre with an air of patron-, age, as if to command were more familiar to him than to obey. It was Constant, *maître d'hôtel* and confidential servant of the Cornelli family for more than fifty years—a Catholic in profession, in heart a Cornelli; that is to say, there was no power on earth, be it cardinal or pope, he would have minded braving in his master's defence; for in that he placed the whole duty of Jean Constant.

"Ah! Monsieur Jean," said Pierre, as he wiped his lips with the cuff of his coat, "this cider reminds me of the day when mademoiselle was christened, and all the tenants and *ouvriers* yonder were supped at monseigneur's expense; it is your prime stingo, this!"

"You may say so," replied Constant, smiling. "I got it up for the especial drinking of the Comte de Pontorson, and he is no bad judge of ciders, I warrant ye."

The other servants joined in a laugh at the comte's expense, but Pierre, suddenly recollecting himself, replied gravely—

"Mon Dieu! to think that we should be here making fun of the sins and follies of that young profligate—laughing at the probable damnation

—the eternal damnation, if you please—of an immortal soul! Ma foi! God forgive us all such levity!"

"Corbleu! Monsieur Pierre," cried Constant, laughing, "I know not if Monsieur le Comte is on the damnation list or no; but this I do know, that while you are preaching on his sins, my best cider is flowing away down a Huguenot gullet!"

A hearty, ringing laugh greeted this sally of the old steward, and Pierre, with a humorous twinkle of the eye, replied—

"Eh bien! mes amis, we must all try to keep temptation away from our weak brethren; the more old Pierre drinks of this vile liquor, so much the less will there be to muddle the brain of Monsieur de Pontorson—but, seriously, who ever saw me the worse for liquor?"

"There spoke a good comrade," answered Constant; "ventre-bleu! wine is for drinking, and no one ever knew thee anything but a wiser and a merrier boy for thy cups, good Pierre; for the smack of the red liquor quenches the smell of the brimstone that thou carriest about thee to fling at good Catholics."

The sound of wheels on the gravel outside scattered the listening group of servants, who

hastily disposed themselves on either side of
the hall to receive with due formality the Comte
de Pontorson.   The sieur himself, too, was on
the steps, ready to welcome his guest, who, after
leaving some injunctions to his servants regarding the four black horses, whose steaming coats
dimmed the light of the lanterns held by the
grooms, ascended the stone steps two at a time,
received the sieur's welcome with a smile that
showed a fine set of teeth and a handsome face,
a little aged by dissipation.

No sooner had the count entered the château than the old hall, whose walls had lately
only echoed to subdued voices and measured
steps, now resounded with the loud and hearty
laughter of the new guest, as he disencumbered
himself of his rugs and wrappers.   The count's
valet, too, bustled about his master's person
with an approving smile at each merry flash of
rough good-humour ; he could not help looking
now and then out of the corners of his laughing
eyes at the sieur's servants who lingered about
the count's luggage, as much as to say, " Yes,
mes braves garçons, here we are ! full of fun as
usual, and meaning to enjoy life and health, and
wine and viands, in spite of your Calvinistic
sourness ;" and the spirit of good-humour

caught fire and spread from the grave *maître d'hôtel* himself to the little scullery girl who came from the kitchen to peep unseen at the company.

Philippe came running downstairs to greet his god-father, for so he persisted in calling the count. He threw himself into the count's arms and kissed him on both cheeks.

"Mon Dieu, Phil! you grow like a girl, with your pale face, and blue eyes, and yellow hair; and, bless my soul! you don't weigh as much as my saddle!" So saying he lifted the boy high above his head.

"I am no girl, god-father, for all that! By-the-by, where's that pony you promised to give me on my birth-day?"

"Pony, eh? Why, here it is, to be sure. Mind you don't slip over his head; he's rather an awkward beast."

So saying, he dropped Philippe astride on the back of his valet, who was stooping to uncord some packages. The sudden weight of the boy made the servant lose his balance, and the valet and Philippe rolled over together on the floor amid general merriment. At this moment a portly figure appeared on the scene, dressed in cassock and black silk stockings.

His face, which was smooth, round, and rubicund, was just then cracked across, as if by a crater, by a quiet but appreciative grin at the horse-play that was going on. He approached the count and saluted him with a bow, still wearing the irrepressible crater from ear to ear.

"Ah, Father Beauvais, quel malheur! Hey, there! somebody fetch a surgeon; the good père has dislocated his jaw, and will never be able to say mass again with a grave face."

The père chuckled very quietly, appearing to laugh especially with his stomach, which struggled dangerously against the barrier of a stout cord which encircled it. At last he gasped out—

"Come, my friend, you kill me! Let me lead you to your apartments. See my time-piece—the cook will chide our delay;" and he led the count up the staircase.

Meanwhile, the servants were preparing supper in the large dining-hall, which lay on the left side of the entrance-hall as you entered the château. Large flaming flambeaux affixed to iron socketsin the walls redeemed the chamber from darkness, and lit up with grim lines of light and shade the full-length portraits of the

Cornelli family, handed down from father to son. At the further end of the hall, on a daïs a little raised, was placed a table at right angles to the large table which occupied the body of the hall. This smaller table the family were used to employ when the number of guests was small enough to admit of it. It was now covered with a white cloth, and Jean Constant had just placed the chief cover on the table, and had given three pulls at a bell rope which was hanging at one corner of the hall. The bell, which rumour said had been abstracted by the sieur's grandfather from the chapel of Mont St. Michel, tolled three in the entrance hall in deep collegiate tones, leaving an echo which seemed to melt away into a higher note, suggestive of far-off wailing. But this might have been fancy, for as the rafters were still thrilling with the sound, the voice of the Comte de Pontorson was heard loud and hearty, and at the same moment he appeared, leading by the hand Madame de Cornelli, arrayed in purple velvet and lace. Behind them came Ethel, who walked by the side of the Père Beretti, but leaving a decent interval between herself and the holy father ; then came De Cornelli himself, leading his daughter by the hand, and at their

side, but a trifle behind them, came the worthy
confessor, Father Beauvais.

When they were all arranged at the table,
ready to take their seats, at a signal from the
sieur, Father Beauvais said a Latin grace, after
which they all crossed themselves three times,
'not omitting the sieur himself. This action
was not unnoticed by Beretti, who just elevated
his eyebrows and busied himself with the deli-
cacies on the table. As he sat on the left hand
of madame he began to question her on the
condition of the poor in her district; then she
gave him a glowing account of her afternoon's
work in a neighbouring hamlet, where the
substantial stone-walls of the cottages only concealed from view the miserable squalor that
prevailed within.

"Ah, my father, those terrible stone-walls
remind me of the barriers of society; they
prevent us from seeing the misery of our poor,
and how often debar us from feeling and rendering sympathy! How often would ladies in
our position be glad to comfort and help their
sisters in misfortune, if they only knew the
depth of *la misère!*"

"Alas, madame! the stone-wall lies, I fear,
in the selfishness of the human heart; our

court ladies turn away in disgust at the sound
of poverty, and your country dames, I doubt
not, though they know how the poor suffer, are
unwilling to trouble themselves.   Ah, madame!
if our Church could number many such devotees
as your ladyship, we should soon hear the last
of ' the religion.' "

Madame coloured a little, and was about to
deprecate the spiritual compliment, when Father
Beauvais, leaning across the table, cried out—

" This is the second time, madame, if you
will allow me to make so bold as to say so, that
the baked pike has been done to cinders : in all
my life I never knew anything so vexatious ! It
is a waste of good viands, madame, which our
good Lady of Grace provides for us ; it is to my
mind almost a sin to overdo a fish of so rare
a quality.   I marvel at the recurrence of this
calamity, madame."

" Good father, I must crave your kind indul-
gence for the cook ; I sent him down to the
village with some broth for my poor, and supper
was provided by his assistants."

" I thought so, madame ; I thought so all
along. Ah ! when shall we learn that the meanest
duties are never too mean to be neglected, that
each has his proper, divinely appointed sphere :

the cook to his fish, the lady to the ordering of her château, the curé to his poor; let but one neglect his proper sphere and all goes wrong."

The poor lady, whose face had just been glowing with pleasure at the thought of having laboured for Christ and his Church, now shrank into silence at the rebuke of her confessor; her eyes were filling with tears, a lump was rising in her throat. Father Beretti, disgusted at the sensuality of his brother priest, and ashamed that the sieur should witness it, bit his lips. Ethel looked across the table, and, meeting the eye of the sieur, saw a gleam of humour twinkling there; she glanced at Marie, and saw the dark eyebrows contracted and the pupil dilating with anger. Ethel thought she knew now why the lord of De l'Esprit did not object to the presence of Father Beauvais. As for the Comte de Pontorson, he had scarcely said half a dozen words all supper time, and looking up with red eyes, swollen with exposure to the cold or by recent libations of cider, he exclaimed—

" By St. Peter! I think the pike a very good pike. Madame, I drink to your health; I wish I had as good a heart as you have. I should need no Father Beauvais then. I think

sending broth to the poor is a very fine thing—
the straight road for heaven ; what do you say,
M. Je'suite ? "

The comte, as he stammered out these words,
extended a cup of cider to Beretti with so
trembling a hand that some of the liquor fell
from the cup : the sieur rose and gave the
signal for grace, which Beauvais repeated in a
mumbling, discontented tone of voice. As· the
comte stopped to finish another cup of wine,
the sieur gave his hand to madame and quitted
the hall. The rest followed, with the exception
of the comte.

" Do we hunt to-morrow in your lord's
woods ? " asked the comte, again replenishing
his glass.

" Assuredly, monseigneur—the huntsman has
orders to be in the home park at eleven ; the
ladies, too, will attend, and the English demoiselle
will ride to hounds."

" En effet ! then must I drink no more of
the brown cider, Constant, lest I disgrace my
country."

So saying, he took his valet's arm and
staggered to bed.

CHAPTER III.

THERE had been a white frost, and the gossamer
threads that interlaced tree with tree and made
the long grass a net-work of silver were shining
in the morning sun when the party of hunters
left the château for the *rendezvous* in the home
park.   Philippe rode first, on a brown pony—he
had exchanged his purple doublet for one of
green ; the hat and the *aigrette* were black.
Maintenon bounded by his side, but the horn
on this occasion was not allowed, lest his ama-
teur too-tooings should interfere with the working of the hounds.   After him came a carriage
drawn by two horses, in which·were Madame de
Cornelli and Father Beauvais.   The carriage
was protected by a roof above, and by curtains
which could be drawn at the sides; but this
morning they were open.   Behind rode the
Comte de Pontorson, also dressed in a doublet

of green, and at his side rode Marie on her white palfrey, wearing a black sash crossed over one shoulder, which contrasted prettily with the green riding-dress that almost touched the ground. The sieur rode next on a powerful chestnut, and it needed all his strength to keep it from breaking away.

Ethel rode a fine black mare, one of the sieur's own breeding; she was the only one of the party not dressed in green, for though Marie had offered to lend her a hunting suit, she had refused it with a kind of horror, as being too gaudy, and had chosen a skirt of black. The sieur looked a little nervously towards her at starting, not feeling sure whether the black mare, which was a young one, would not be too much for the *gouvernante*. But the light, firm hand and easy seat which she displayed at the first playful bound of her steed set him at ease on that score.

Behind their master rode Pierre and four grooms, carrying the materials for lunch, and leading two fresh horses. Pierre was this morning unusually light-hearted, and with difficulty subdued the tones of his voice to a half-audible murmur. He was chanting, this merry spring morning; but his chaunt was not of the usual pious ring, but seemed to be of a merry friar who robbed the Church and rode a-hunting. One of the grooms had the ill-luck to interrupt him in the middle of a stanza—

"Parbleu! Monsieur Pierre, we shall soon be riding to church! See you how the young mistress pairs off with the gay gallant yonder?"

"Fi donc! Fi donc! What an arrant ass thou art to speak so loud, even in thy master's hearing! I vow thou hast tempted me to make use of some ill-mouthed oath, thou scurvy varlet! What canst thou know of ladies and gallants?—thou that wast born in a pig-stye and bred amongst Breton goats! Now, hark ye, Master François, just to put an embargo on that clattering tongue of thine, I will throw a ray of light on thy clouded understanding. Why, thou Jack-fool! didst not see last night how my lord plied Monseigneur le Comte with his strong cider? Do men make their guests drunk in order to set them off to the best advantage? or, dost think Mademoiselle Marie would like a suitor any the better for making a beast of himself in her presence? Faugh! mon François, thou must to school again, I fear."

"Ah, Monsieur Pierre, thou speakest like a

priest—glib and unintelligible. Thou art like a mass-book, where all is Latin; thou shouldst have been a curé thyself, for thou canst throw in a mass of arguments enough to bewilder a whole parish — thou art too clever for poor François, who, for his part, would give his best cider to the man who was going to marry his daughter, and if he got drunk on it, why, would look upon it as a compliment to the cellar."

"Ay, thou speakest after the fashion of the kitchen, where guzzling and drinking are the main pleasures of life, and where a little excess, more or less, is lightly atoned for by the fingering of your beads. But know, for all that, Master François, that thou wilt surely be damned!"

This sally of temper and theology on the part of Pierre only raised a bitter smile on the part of the grooms, who had been pressing round to listen to the discussion. They were Catholics; but a full license of speech was always allowed old Pierre, on the ground of his master's favour, and his many good qualities.

Meanwhile the cavalcade had reached a part of the forest where the ground had been cleared of trees, and a farm-house and a few stacks redeemed the solitude of the spot. On the greensward in front of the cottage was gathered a group of the sieur's huntsmen, some on foot and some mounted, and lying on the grass or rolling over one another were clustered the hounds that were to find sport for the day. They were not all of one breed, for the stag-hound was mixed with a sort of beagle, while three or four smooth terriers were held in leashes by the huntsmen. A few rustics in their blue blouses were attracted to the meet, and except these the field was strictly confined to the members of the sieur's household.

All uncovered respectfully as the sieur and his party approached; and after a few words of greeting to the old man who hobbled out on crutches to the door of the cottage, the sieur raised his hat, and the head-huntsman unslung his horn. But in the mean time there seemed to be some strong manifestations of feeling on the part of the hounds, who were encircling and keeping at bay some creature in their midst. Ethel and Philippe rode up to the scene of the *émeute*, and beheld Maintenon standing with his head and tail thrown up, and with a look of ineffable disdain thrown into his whole body; which feeling, however, was shown to be a youthful affectation by the careful outlook he maintained from the corners of his eyes. The hounds were evidently somewhat suspicious of the gigantic intruder, who growled a low and lordly growl, as much as to say, ' Touch me if you dare.' At the first blast of the horn Maintenon was released from the curious sniffs of his inquisitors, who broke away over the beady turf with quivering tails and lowered heads. For some time they rode up and down the numerous avenues in the forest, some of which were wide enough for the carriage to follow, others again so narrow that the riders could only proceed in single file. Sometimes they came out into open spaces, glades between the forests of greensward, and again they would enter a dark plantation of fir, where there was no underwood to impede the riders, and the sandy soil yielded and the fallen branches cracked under the hoofs of the hunters.

" Does not this remind you of your cathedrals at home, mademoiselle?" said the sieur to Ethel, as he pointed to the long, columnar row of pines and the boughs that overarched them ; then, speaking solemnly, he added—

" This is my church. Here I love to wander alone and commune with the God of Nature, of

Peace, of Love; here I can lift up my heart to God and give free utterance to the thoughts that rise within me, and feel that I am talking direct to my Father—that there is no iron hand of authority drawn across my lips to smother the thoughts which are truth to me because I feel them true. Yes, mademoiselle, it is here only—in the still and unfrequented haunts of the wild fox and the stag—that I can feel that no human figure stands between me and my Heavenly Father, commanding me to believe this doctrine, and to reject that, under pain of eternal punishment. See how yon sunlight glints through the thick branches of the pine forest, and silvers the gnarled roots sparsely here and there. So the divine light filters through the cumbersome overgrowth of human tradition and Church ceremonial; but give me the clear sunlight full upon my face, beating direct from the throne of God upon the natural instincts of my heart! Yea! I will stand and gaze upon it, though its very brightness blind me."

"I thought," answered Ethel, "that the French Reformed were very much under the spiritual guidance of Calvin."

"Ah! you strike home there, mademoiselle.

It is too true that our brethren of the Reformed
have exchanged the authority of Rome for that
of Geneva; they have shaken their consciences
free of the Pope only to bind them beneath the
sway of a French lawyer. However, we cannot
expect slaves to be fit for freedom at a blow;
much has been gained to them by the exchange
of masters, and we must leave it to time,
education, the fuller knowledge of Christ, to do
the rest."

"Then, monsieur, you do not rank yourself
with the Calvinists?" said Ethel, who was
curious to know what were the opinions of her
companion.

"With them, certainly; of them, no! I will
strike with them for freedom, for liberty of conscience, and the Bible, but I will not be compelled to follow them in their narrow dogmatism
on questions not religious."

At this moment there was a rustling in the
greenwood, and a gallant stag bounded out into
the clear forest and was gone in a few seconds;
at the same time the deep bell-tones of an old
hound proclaimed the fact to the whole pack,
and from all sides the dogs came pushing
through the brushwood, casting about beneath
the fir-trees for the scent, and suddenly sweep-

ing into the traces of the stag, as a stream of water is swept into a sloping channel. De Cornelli sounded a blast on his horn—" They are off! dare you follow, or will you return to the ladies ? "

Ethel had no time to answer, for the black mare had made her decision as soon as she caught sight of the hounds, and would not be gainsaid. It was rather nervous work threading in and out amongst the firs ; but fortunately they grew thinner and thinner, and now daylight could be seen ahead, and something which looked like a hedge as they approached it. Ethel saw that the carriage had already drawn up ; the comte and Marie, too, were reining in their horses, and two servants in livery were trying to make a gap in the hedge. They shouted as the sieur and Ethel approached, and pointed to the hedge in a deprecating way ; De Cornelli seemed to waver, and was pulling in, when the black mare, with a little scream of defiance, shot ahead and took the fence in fine style. An exclamation of wonder and relief broke from the little group beside the hedge, who had looked to see a catastrophe. Cornelli himself, with a " Mon Dieu !" followed in Ethel's wake ; the comte, whose French pride was touched by the superior riding of the *demoiselle Anglaise*, craved permission to leave the ladies, and the powerful stride of his hunter soon laid him alongside the other two.

For more than a mile the three rode at a hand-gallop over an undulating expanse of furze-patched grass, with no obstacles to surmount, save now and then a tiny stream ; the hounds were a good half mile in front, though there were several stragglers labouring far in the rear ; the huntsman's horn rang out incessantly and distinctly in the clear air, making the shepherd stand agape as he leaned on his crook, and the girl pause in her spinning and forget the brindled cow she came out to tend. But at length the furze and the broom and the green carpet over which the horses sprang with so buoyant a step came to an end, and the ground beyond them began to spread out like a patch-work counterpane, yellow and green and red. Away pounded the count through clover and carrots, trifolium and the tender wheat, his eyes fixed on the now straggling pack and the stag which staggered not many paces in front of the leading hound. But not so rode the Sieur de Cornelli, who, shouting in vain to his guest to avoid the cultured crops, had directed Ethel to follow him by a slight *détour* where a cart-track led through·the cultivated plots.

"They are the property of the poor cottiers; let us avoid the plots."

"I see a village," cried Ethel, "and the stag seems to have run into a farm-yard; see, what a crowd of people!"

And the two rode down a gentle slope, the foam breaking from the nostrils of their steeds and floating away behind them, or splashing the rider with occasional flakes. They were nearing the little cluster of farm-house and cottages. The hounds were braying round the chief entrance, the door of which seemed to be shut, and the huntsmen were struggling, whip in hand, to keep the pack off; a crowd of men, women, and children were gesticulating and shouting and laughing; furniture lay scattered about on the grass on all sides; a man, a woman, and four little children, sat moodily, in strange contrast to the noisy excitement of the rest, upon the boxes that were piled up, or lay chaotic amongst supine tables and horizontal chairs. As the sieur's horse clattered on the stones that paved the road in front of the house there was a momentary hush of voices, and caps were doffed and curtseys dropped; then an old man, stepping forward, explained, in a hurried manner—

" Excuse me, monseigneur, we are selling off to-day the goods of ce monsieur là bas—he who sits on yon boxes; eh, bien! what do we hear but your lordship's horn sounding over the hill-side, and then *tout à coup* comes your lordship's stag, right into the centre of the ring, knocks down his majesty's servant, who was conducting the sale, and vanishes into the farm-house. Ah! monseigneur, mais c'est si drôle!"

" Et après? The stag, where is it now?" asked Cornelli.

" Ah! the stag! that is what I was going to tell monseigneur."

At this point the pent-up feelings of the listening crowd could be contained no longer; a fury of babbling tongues lashed out in explanation of the consequences, and so clamorous were the crowd in their eagerness to tell the story, that it was impossible to understand their meaning; only the words, "Pasteur"—"la porte fermée," were repeated again and again.

" Gently, my friends, gently, if you please— one at a time. Come, Master André, keep thy good people quiet, and tell me all about it."

The person addressed, a little man in a braided military coat and cocked hat, who was there to represent the king's justice—the tax-collector and public functionary of the district—now stepped forward and rang a little hand-bell, crying, in a shrill voice—

" Messieurs et mesdames, grand silence ! Monseigneur wishes to hear the true account of the lost stag. Silence there, you boys! how dare you laugh in the . face of his majesty's collector of taxes ! "

This last remark was uttered with some warmth to a group of *gamins*, who, forgetting the proper respect due to a government official, were imitating the cries of various animals in a low tone of voice. Then, bringing his hand up to the military salute, M. André, red with anger and swollen with self-importance, began to speak—

" Monseigneur will pardon me if I call his attention to this battered hat and soiled coat, the result of a severe blow from monseigneur's stag."

Here a smile passed over the faces in the crowd, like a gleam of sunshine gliding over a field of wheat ; and it was curious to observe how those immediately in front of the officer tried to conceal it by coughing and rubbing their chins.

"Monseigneur will take notice that I, Jean André, am here to-day to fulfil a government duty—however unpleasant to myself, yet necessary to the interests of the State ; and it cannot be allowed that sympathy with the evicted cottier should endanger the life of his majesty's servants, lawfully engaged in a necessary yet painful duty."

"Saint Michael and all the holy angels ! " broke in the Comte de Pontorson, slapping his riding-boot with the long handle of his whip. "What the devil do we care about you and your dirty grievances ! Produce the stag, man, if you haven't eaten it, or I'll quicken your intelligence ! "

De Cornelli interposed in a courteous manner between the impatient nobleman and the astounded tax-collector, observing—

"I am equally anxious with Monseigneur the Comte de Pontorson to learn quickly what you have done with the poor beast."

At the mention of the count's name there was a stir of surprise and several hats were raised. André was about to answer, when an upper window was flung open in the old farm-house, and a grey-headed old man, attired in black, and wearing large Geneva bands round his neck, leaned half out, and waving his hand, said, in a deep, quiet voice—

" It is I, monseigneur, who have shut the door against your huntsmen, and have hitherto saved the life of a poor hunted beast. In the name of the God of Mercy, I ask you to deliver from death a creature that hath shown wit enough to fly for shelter to a human habitation."

A scornful laugh burst from the bystanders ; the huntsmen gave vent to indignant murmurs ; the count uttered an oath.

Ethel looked at the sieur, and seemed to plead for the stag.

The *gamins* were muttering between their teeth, " *À bas les pasteurs !* "

This saved the life of the poor beast. De Cornelli, glancing round with flashing eyes, ordered silence on pain of instant imprisonment.

" I will not allow the officer of the Intendant to be interrupted in his duty. Let the sale recommence — huntsmen, draw off your dogs. Monsieur la Rose, your plea for mercy is heard. Monseigneur, I am sorry the day's sport has come to so sudden a termination, but you will allow that we have given you a good gallop."

The comte laughed and shrugged his shoulders, and drawing from his pocket a pipe of tobacco, proceeded to strike a light on a flint, which he carried suspended on the chain which also guarded a gold chronometer. The process of striking a light and kindling the tobacco was watched with curious interest by the peasants, to whom tobacco was as yet an unknown luxury. Meanwhile the pasteur had come out of the cottage, and was engaged in conversation with the Sieur de Cornelli.

He was a tall, thin, but apparently vigorous old man, and his white hair, which flowed in long curls beneath the broad-brimmed *chapeau*, made him look older than he really was. His face, when in repose, was somewhat stern, seared with numerous curving lines about the mouth, and embrowned by constant exposure to the . weather. Two dark lines running where the whiskers usually grow showed that an occasional use of the razor was resorted to ; when the old man smiled, his face ran itself readily into the said curving lines, like a jelly into a mould, showing that the merry view of life had been constant enough to photograph itself upon his features.

Presently, as André was holding up a mirror for the inspection of purchasers, De Cornelli advanced and said—

"Monsieur Jean André, it is now needless for you to go on with the sale of Guillebert's property, for in consequence of statements which have been made to me by Monsieur le Pasteur"—as the sieur paused a minute to look round, the assembled peasants and tradesmen shuffled closer, old men sheltered the wind from their ears with eager lifting of the hand, and some turned to beckon to the forlorn group that squatted amongst the *débris* of furniture—"In consequence of those statements, I repeat, and in sincere sympathy for our poor friend Guillebert, who, I presume you are all aware, is reduced to this distress by no fault of his, but simply and solely from the unjust and shameful method of taxation which prevails in this unfortunate country, whereby the whole burden is laid upon the working-classes—I say, in consequence of this injustice I, the Sieur de Cornelli, as seigneur of this district, deem it my duty to share and lighten the burden of taxation which presses so heavily on the cultivators of the soil. I therefore discharge the debt due by Guillebert to the State, and call upon you, my friends, to do your part by restoring to the owner the several articles you may already have bought at the sale. You have my word for it that no one shall suffer any loss in this matter."

With difficulty had the last few words been listened to, so eager had the crowd become to applaud the generous and unexpected speech of the sieur ; but when at last he paused, hats and *vivats* were thrown into the air, and four or five stalwart young men ran to fetch Guillebert to his benefactor.

Meanwhile Pierre held his master's stirrup whilst he dismounted, but there was a look of mild disapproval in the old servitor's face, as he managed to whisper, " Excuse me, does monseigneur not know that this Guillebert here is a bigoted Catholic ? Is it possible ? "

And now there came, dragged along by a crowd of congratulating peasants, the unfortunate owner of the farm-house. He was a head taller than any one else, and stout in proportion ; his dress was that of a peasant ; he wore a long blouse reaching nearly to the knee, his legs were encased in tight-fitting gaiters, his head was bare. He did not show any signs of joy at the news his friends had brought him ; his aspect was that of a man whom misfortune had crushed, and whose wits were not keen enough to grasp so sudden a turn of fortune. He came up to his patron with an uncertain step and dazed eyes, made his bow, and began to stammer out some excuse for his misfortunes.

"Ah! monseigneur, my family have held this little farm for three generations—three generations! and it is I who have disgraced my name. Yet, monseigneur, I should have kept my head above water, if they had not assessed me far beyond my means. And then, again, it was the confiscation of my last year's growth of cider, because my head-labourer stole the money I gave him to pay the king's dues. Ah! that was the blow that first made me tremble.. You see, my friends, I had no money to buy manure for my land, nothing to pay the *taille* from—*et puis*, monseigneur, the tax-collector has sold all. And what is to become of poor Jeanne and the children?"

The strong man burst into tears and buried his face in his hands. There were many soiled handkerchiefs applied to wet eyes in sympathy with the honest cottier, and a few moments of silence followed, only broken by the sobs of the women. At length De Cornelli, placing his hand on the shoulder of Guillebert, who stood looking on the ground, said—

"Come, come, my friend, don't give way to despair! Your name, your honour, is not tarnished in Normandy. What though the king's ministers have made the taxes too heavy for some of us to bear! Remember, my friends, all of you who are here, that there are two classes in the social order who pay no taxes—the clergy and the nobility. It is the duty—yea, it is the proud privilege—of these two orders to come to the assistance of those who are overburdened. Guillebert, you and I are both free Normans; accept, then, the help it is my duty to render you. Nay, man, do not kneel to thank me; in God's sight we are equal, and it is in the name of God's justice that I pay your debts and restore to you, your wife, and children, and this farm unencumbered."

Guillebert was on his knees, sobbing and kissing the sieur's hand. "It is too kind, too forgiving, monseigneur, after the annoyance and opposition I have always raised against my lord. I shall never forget it—no, never! Here, Jeanne, my sweet, bring the little ones and thank monseigneur for all his goodness."

Then the wife came with the corner of her white apron in her eye, crying and laughing by turns, while two little girls of five and six years, whom she led by the hand, were looking up intently and watching the varying changes of their mother's face, and imitating the laughter and the tears with accurate fidelity. They were evidently impressed with the gravity of the occasion, determined not to be more than a few seconds behindhand in the expression of their feelings; but what those feelings meant, or why they were evoked, was beyond their tiny ken. However, all were soon merrily at work replacing the furniture in the house.

The carriage had by this time driven up with madame and Father Beauvais; Marie, too, had rejoined Ethel, and there was quite a gay assembly chatting and laughing over the merry turn of circumstances.

"A day commenced after the flesh, with hunting and worldly thoughts of pleasure, completed after the Spirit, with a work of Christian charity," said a voice near the carriage.

Madame turned, and recognized the aged Protestant pasteur with a formal bend of the head. The old man made a low and respectful bow, and, approaching the confessor, said, in a whisper—

"Pardon me, M. Beauvais, if I interfere in this matter; but 'monseigneur has been led to speak of the duties of the clergy and of the harshness of the king's ministers somewhat too boldly, perhaps ; and—but you will pardon me, I know—I have just seen one of your priests, in disguise, running off with his account of it, no doubt, into Coutances."

" Thank you, M. le Pasteur," replied Father Beauvais, nodding his head and indulging in an unclerical wink at his heretical friend ; " thank you for your caution ; I will see the wretch does no mischief."

" What says the pasteur ? " inquired madame, haughtily.

" Oh ! ah ! why—a—he thinks the Guilleberts will want a little ready money, without doubt."

" To be sure, my father ; make a memorandum of it, lest I forget. These people are good Catholics, I believe. What does Monsieur la Rose amongst them ? Ma foi ! this acquittal should have come from me."

" Oh, fear not that monseigneur will make converts of them ; that is not his *rôle*. Strange ! how he lives the life of Christ, in all respects save in obeying and conforming to His Church. He is all charity, and nothing else ! "

" Ah ! it is very, very sad ! " sighed madame, turning away to hide a tear.

On the evening of the day we have just described, there was a bright fire blazing in the private study of Monseigneur the Bishop of Coutances. The red curtains had been carefully drawn across the windows to exclude the chill night air, a heavy piece of antique tapestry hung on a brass rod and intercepted intruding breezes from the door, and the ponderous tomes that filled the book-cases on three sides of the chamber gave forth a genial glimmer from their burly backs, lettered with gold. The table which filled the centre of the room was littered with manuscripts and bundles of letters tied together with tape ; some were lying torn upon the polished oak floor, together with the string by which they had been tied. On the chimney-piece stood a chronometer ; it was the model of a cathedral, and a solitary hand on the dial in one of the towers gave notice of the march of minutes, and left the observer to discover the hour for himself. Seated in a large arm-chair by the fire, with a small round table by his side, was a priest of about forty-five years ; his hair was raven black, his face close shaven, his forehead high, the nose aquiline, the mouth curved. It would have been a handsome face had the cheeks not been somewhat sunken, and the

brow contracted into a perpetual frown by study.
As it was, the fine, well-cut features, and kind,
melancholy expression made it an interesting
face. At this moment the bishop, for he it was,
with both elbows on the table, was perusing
a letter he had just written; he proceeded to
fold it up, and was holding a wax taper in one
hand and a lump of wax in the other when a
tap was heard at the door. At the bishop's
bidding a young boy entered, clad in a long
serge robe.

"There is a priest without, monseigneur, who
would speak with you; he is a Benedictine—
one of those who came from Paris with Father
Beretti."

"It is late for such a visitor; however, bid
him enter, dear boy;" and the bishop, perhaps
with some idea of adding an appearance of age,
hastily placed on his head a black skull-cap.

A monk then entered the bishop's apartment,
thrusting aside the tapestry and peering in
cautiously before entering. He saluted the
bishop.

"Good evening, Brother Francis, you find
me busy with my papers to-night."

"I am sorry to interrupt monseigneur, but I
bring a letter of importance."

So saying, he fumbled in a pouch that was attached to his girdle; as he did so, the dark lustrous eyes of the bishop seemed to scan him through and through. His face, pitted with the small-pox and covered with red blotches, his straight brown hair, his deep-set, inquisitively restless eyes, his thick lips and massive chin, all came under episcopal scrutiny; and the curving lines of the bishop's mouth grew straighter and straighter, and the melancholy tenderness of his gaze seemed to be changing into a look of concentrated firmness, as he watched the Benedictine unfold his letter.

"Ah!" exclaimed the bishop, as he ran his eye over the letter; "a few lines from our friend Beretti, to tell me you have an affair of weight to disclose."

"Precisely, M. l'Évêque;—something that concerns your own diocese."

"Pray take that seat, Brother Francis; I am listening."

The monk glanced round the room and began with downcast eyes :—

"An errand of mercy, monseigneur, had carried me into the neighbourhood of a farm belonging to Monsieur Guillebert, a staunch Catholic, as is well known. To my surprise, I noticed a large crowd gathered in front of the house, and on approaching, I discovered that Monsieur André was selling off the cottier's effects for debts due to the king. Almost at that moment the Sieur de l'Esprit, M. de Cornelli, a Huguenot, as monseigneur well knows, began to make a violent speech against the king's ministers and the members of our holy order, accusing the former of injustice and the latter of indifference to their duty; and the more to inflame the people, he on the spot offered to pay all Guillebert's debts—an offer which, of course, drew forth the *vivats* of the Catholics present—and—and—I think I need not say more to convince monseigneur of the evil tendency which——"

"Brother Francis, you have said quite enough. There are not many priests like you, I believe, in my diocese——"

"Pardon me, monseigneur, I cannot listen to words of praise ; my vows——"

"Ma foi! you interrupt me!" replied the bishop, in a sharp tone, which made the smiling, self-complacent features of the monk change on a sudden to an expression of cunning watchfulness ; he now glanced sideways at the fire. "Answer me one or two questions, brother, and take care you speak as accurately as if you were making your confession: now, first, on what errand of mercy were you employed this morning when you drew near this sale?"

The Benedictine looked up surprised, fumbled with his crucifix, and said nothing.

The bishop slowly took a letter from a packet which lay on the table, and read aloud—

"'À M. le Secrétaire Intime de l'Évêque—The Sieur of Mont-Vert has the honour to invite the bishop's secretary to a *déjeûner* at eleven o'clock to meet the Benedictine Frère Francis.' Were you there, brother?"

" I was, monseigneur, but——"

"Excuse me," interrupted the bishop, and rang a silver hand-bell.

"Send M. le Secrétaire to me at once, if you please."

In a few minutes appeared a little priest in large tortoise-shell spectacles.

"At what time did you and Brother Francis leave the *déjeûner* this morning?"

" I left at one, and Brother Francis remained, as he was, he said, at leisure."

" I thank you—that will do;" and the secretary bowed and retired.

The bishop took up another letter; it was

from Father Beauvais, giving an account of the
sale, and the exact words used by De Cornelli,
and stating the precise time, "half-past one."

"So much, Brother Francis, for your errand of
mercy! A party of pleasure, and on your road
home, I presume, the *espionnage*—but, sir, the
one lie shakes your credit as to the testimony to
the violent language of the sieur; let us see!"
and the bishop read aloud Father Beauvais's
letter.

"I hope, brother," he resumed, "you do not
include all the clergy in your damnatory con-
clusions. You observe that what the sieur said
was, 'It is the duty—yea, the proud privilege—
of the clergy to help the over-burdened;' and
what you report is, 'he accused the clergy of
indifference to their duty.' Now, brother, it may
be that a stricken conscience, brooding over the
sieur's words, may have led to an involuntary
mis-statement——"

"It was that, monseigneur, it was that!"
eagerly broke in the monk.

"Oh, very well! then you escape the terrible
charge of a double lie, but you confess to bearing a conscience so convinced of neglect of
religious duties, that the very messages of truth
you hear from other men's lips become trans-

muted in your sinful, worldly heart, into messages of hate and falsehood. Ah, brother, brother! when will you learn that he who fights with the weapons of this world shall perish by those weapons! You have been tempted— tempted by a feeling of *esprit de corps*—to commit two grievous sins: you have played the devil's part, and have slandered a good man— nay! start not; heretic though he be, the Sieur de Cornelli is a good man. Go! pray God to give you a new heart, and a deeper love of truth; it is not a cowl or a tonsure that keeps us unspotted. Go! cleanse thine house of its demons of malice and falsehood, and may our Lady intercede for thee with Him who reads our hearts!"

The Benedictine turned a baffled look to his superior and quitted the room. When, a few minutes after this, an old lady wearing a tall Norman cap entered the study with a bowl of smoking *bouillon*, she found the bishop on his knees beside the table, his crucifix grasped tightly between his folded hands, his head sunk on the table.

She placed the soup near him, and stole on tip-toe to the fire, glancing round nervously at times to the kneeling figure.

The bishop, absorbed in prayer, noticed nothing—it was a struggle with Satan, that prayer of his! Sobs and convulsive cries shook his whole frame; sometimes words escaped him —"' And they all forsook Him, and fled.' Oh! non, non, jamais, mon Seigneur, forsake not thy church—oh! for peace, for charity!" And the sobs and prayer at last ended in a passionate burst of tears.

The old lady went to him, and put her arm round his neck. "Tenez, mon fils, mon cher fils! thy prayer is heard; trust in the good God. There, there, put thy poor head on thy mother's breast; there, poor boy, on thy mother's breast, and I mine on the good Lord's." And so the good old lady rocked him, like a child, on her breast, till the convulsive sobs ceased, and stroking her face he fell into a sweet forgetfulness of all his troubles.

CHAPTER IV.

THE morning of Marie's fête-day awoke with a
wreath of mist and fog, through which the sun
now and then thrust a red, inquisitive face, as if
to see how things were going on. The head-
gardener was standing on the high terrace
which overlooked the gardens and their slopes,
and by his side was old Pierre, apparently
giving his opinion on the weather, and pointing
to gleams of sunshine which came slanting
down and touched the tops of the highest
poplars.

Lower down, on the level lawn, were men
engaged in setting up swings and tents, and
flag-staffs bearing gay banners and fluttering
flags ; and at one end of the lawn was a rustic
throne for the Queen of Beauty, who should
give the guerdon of valour to the conqueror in
the mimic tournament ; on the left rose the

maze, its tiny hedges draped with colours, its summit surmounted with the great flag bearing the Cornelli arms.

Marie, in her rose-coloured *peignoir*, was gazing from her bed-room window at the preparations which were being made to celebrate her birthday. On her toilet-table lay some of the presents sent in before she was awake by the hands of her maid. There was a necklace of pearls from her mother, a silver-tipped riding-whip from Philippe, an illuminated Bible from her father, and two or three souvenirs from the old servants, who took this opportunity of showing their respectful affection for their young mistress. There was a little oil-painting, too, of the old church of St. Lô, with a company of marines in the fore-ground, and a gallant officer, about three times the size of his men, whose face was prudently turned away—this was Ethel's gift ; and lastly, there was a beautiful little casket, gold enamelled, with " M. de C." painted in blue letters on the top—the " unworthy contribution of Adolphe, Comte de Pontorson.".

Marie's heart was light, as every Frenchwoman's is on the day of her fête. She was humming to herself a light refrain, when a tap

on the door startled her into silence, and
madame, entering, threw herself affectionately
into her daughter's arms, and kissed her again
and again.   After a few words of congratulation
had passed, the comte's casket caught madame's
eye, and, with a gesture of perhaps feigned
surprise, she took it up and turned it round and
about, and called it "mighty fine."

"I am sorry he has sent it, mamma; I shall
return it."

"Return it, mon enfant? I cannot hear of such
a thing! it would be extremely impolite, and it
would look like affectation in one who has
known Adolphe from her childhood. Why,
Marie, you are but seventeen to-day; you should
not think of such things."

"Ma foi! it is Monsieur le Comte who puts
such things in my head; he was talking nonsense and flattering me all that day we were
out with the hounds."

"He was?" cried madame, flushing with
excitement; "then why did you not tell your
mother at once, you naughty one?"

"I thought it of no consequence," replied
Marie, tossing her head.

"Girls so young as you are can be no fit
judges of what is important. I have known

great mischief follow from secrets between mother and daughter."

" Eh bien, ma mère! one day when we were out walking, M. le Comte suddenly fell on his knees before me, and I ran away."

" Bah! that was just like you again. You should have given him a hearing."

" I shall not marry at all," and Marie began to show symptoms of tears.

"Oh, Marie, darling, forgive me if I have been brusque with you ; but you know marriage cannot happen often in one lifetime, and one must needs be prudent."

" Mais, mamma, you ran away with papa against her Majesty's wishes."

" Yes, my darling, but your papa was so clever and good, and a—— "

" A Huguenot!" said Marie archly, with a tell-tale blush.

Madame de Cornelli, having nothing to say in answer to this unexpected checkmate, bit her lip and said angrily—

" Now, Marie, I warn you seriously that any clandestine correspondence with young Guillot will be regarded unfavourably by your father and myself ; do be cautious, ma chère, for a false step may plunge us all into a serious calamity— now, remember! "

So saying, lifting an admonitory forefinger, madame retired.

There was no more singing that morning in Marie's dressing-room ; her mother's words had roused her natural wilfulness, and as her maid was arranging her *coiffure*, she sat meditating on Lieutenant Henri and the days of childhood which they had passed so merrily together.

At ten o'clock in the forenoon the great bell clanged out in the hall, and the servants in their red livery lined the sides of the dining-hall, awaiting the guests, who, on this occasion, were numerous enough to fill the long table which ran lengthwise down the centre.

Many of the notables of the neighbourhood had already arrived, and the château was full of valets and maids running about in a pretty confusion, with their masters' or mistresses' dresses for the ball which was to take place in the evening. Some of the guests were arriving as the sieur and his friends were passing to the dining-hall.

The Comte de Pontorson had just turned to address a remark to Marie, who should have been pacing demurely at his side, when, to his surprise, he found his partner had escaped, and was at that moment receiving a kiss upon her

upturned brow from a tall, white-headed old
gentleman, whose dark eyes were sparkling
with delight, and with something of the fire of
fifty years ago. By his side stood a young man
in naval uniform, stroking his dark moustache
with one hand, and eyeing the old gentleman's
warm caresses with a humorous twinkle, as
if he were saying to himself, " Ha, ha! monsieur mon père has found a pretty girl as well as
an old friend."

As soon as Marie had disengaged herself
from the old man's embrace she made Lieutenant Henri a ceremonious curtsey, bade him
and his father welcome, and, inviting them to
join the guests at the *déjeûner*, ran off to take
her place at the table.

It was not a formal gathering this morning,
partly because fresh guests constantly arriving
were expected to come in at any moment;
but yet Marie found the company respectfully
standing and waiting for her approach. She
blushed deeply, and as she passed in front of
her mother's chair, dropped a low curtsey and
apologized.

Madame gave her a look full of meaning, and
inclined her head. Father Beauvais, who had
been drumming with his fingers on the table,

and had already tucked a large white napkin under his chin, cried out—

"À la bonne heure, mademoiselle! I thought I had lost you."

"Don't believe the father!—he thought he had lost his *déjeûner!*" shouted a little man, dressed as an ecclesiastic, looking round for applause.

"Ah, that's the Abbé Huet, I will wager an angel! He is always making bad jokes when he is not editing the classics for the Dauphin."

"Yes, messieurs et mesdames, when I want to unbend my mind, I love to watch *le bon père là bas* dip his fingers in the stew-pan: 'dulce est desipere in loco'—Father Beauvais will translate it. He is well up in the fathers. Come now, my friend, your version of it?"

"Abbé Huet, it is not seemly to quote the fathers at such a moment."

A burst of laughter followed this display of ignorance on the part of the confessor.

In the midst of the uproar which had greeted the confessor's speech, Captain and Lieutenant Guillot entered the hall. The sieur at once rose, shook them by the hand and saluted them on the cheek, and then presented them to madame, who sat by his side. They then went down the table shaking hands and bandying words of salutation and welcome with many of the guests to whom they were well known.

Marie soon found means to retire quietly with Ethel, since it was not permitted her to partake of food until she had "made her communion." As she passed through the outer hall, a young priest, looking wistfully through spectacles, approached her and said, in a timid voice—

"If mademoiselle wishes, Monsieur l'Évêque will see her in private."

Marie accepted the guidance of the young secretary to a private chamber, where the bishop was waiting to confer with the fair *communicante*.

Meanwhile many ladies were making their way to the chapel to witness or take part in the religious service which was to usher in the proceedings of the day. Priests in long robes were waiting about, and little acolytes in white vestments with crimson sashes round their waists were busy lighting the candles upon and about the altar. A Jesuit was kneeling on the stone steps leading to the altar, his head bowed in prayer ; a Benedictine, who had sat at table a few minutes before, entered hurriedly, and stepping lightly up to the Jesuit, whispered in his ear. The Jesuit rose, bowed to the altar, and followed the monk out of the chapel.

At the entrance of the chapel, and between the *grilles*, or iron gates, which guarded the arched passage leading to the rest of the château, were gathered a few priests and some of the servants of the guests. The Jesuit, addressing one of the tonsured gentlemen, said—

" Keep these gates partly closed until the procession arrives, and see that no heretic passes more than a few paces into the chapel."

The priest bowed, and obeyed his orders by closing one gate and standing in the way to question all who passed.

Presently a party of gentlemen appeared, laughing merrily with words of banter and fun, gradually dying down into reverent silence as they drew near the iron gates. The priest whispered in the ear of each, and, on receiving a nod in reply, opened the gate and allowed him to pass. At length, as old Captain Guillot approached, the priest quietly closed the other gate, and politely whispered in the old officer's ear—

" Monsieur, il est défendu!" accompanying

the refusal with a slight wave of the hand, and bowing with studied courtesy.

For a moment the old man was staggered; his companions, who had already passed into the chapel, were turning to see what was the cause of the delay, the servants were whispering together and pointing.

"By whose command am I forbidden entrance?" demanded the captain.

The priest bowed, and said a general order had been given to admit only Catholics.

At this moment Philippe made his appearance, and Captain Guillot, accosting him, exclaimed, "You and I are heretics; we may not enter."

"What!" cried Philippe, reddening; "have these priests dared to stop you? I apologize to you, M. le Capitaine. In the name of my father, follow me."

And the little fellow, in all the offended majesty of a dozen years, strutted towards the *grille.* "Ouvrez, s'il vous plaît, monsieur," he exclaimed.

"Certainly," replied the priest, and admitting Philippe, shut out the captain.

"Admit M. le Capitaine instantly, or I report you to my father!"

"It is against orders, my son.   I am very sorry," and again the priest bowed.

A party of ladies were now approaching, and amongst them was madame. As they came near, Philippe cried out, "Is it true, mamma, that only Catholics are permitted to enter the chapel to-day?"

"I know not, mon cher fils; the arrangements are under the control of le Père Beretti," replied madame.

"Ah! le Père Beretti," whispered the servants in the background.

"But I am sure there must be some mistake," continued madame, inclining graciously towards the captain.

"Oh! madame, I should be the last person in the world to rebel against properly constituted authority; allow me to retire," and the captain turned to depart. He now met Father Beauvais, arrayed in splendid vestments, as he was to take part in the service of the mass.

"Hallo! M. le Capitaine, whither away? we are going to begin directly."

"Pardon me, M. le Confesseur—heretics are not allowed by Beretti to enter."

"Vraiment! fi donc! who is this Beretti, to

stop the sieur's friends in his own house?
Come with me, my friend, come with me!"

So saying, he drew his friend's arm through
his own and made straight for the *grille*, afford-
ing to the on-lookers a strange contrast of the
Church and the world linked arm in arm—the
one being stout and puffy and indignant,
the other spare and tall and wearing an air of
amusement.

"Comment! stand aside, M. le Prêtre! en
voilà une affaire! making a disturbance in consecrated ground! let my friend pass instantly."
The priest saluted Father Beauvais silently,
keeping his hand on the gate.

"I tell you, open the gate! By St. Francis,
if it were not for my sacred dress and holy
office, I would put my fingers about thy
scraggy throat!"

"It is impossible. I have received orders
to the contrary."

"I care not for orders, not if the devil himself have given them. Infâme! I trust to make
an example of thee, this day. You will not
open? then, God help you! I *will* be about
thy windpipe."

As he gasped out these choleric words
Father Beauvais made a sudden clutch through

the iron grating at the priest's throat. The latter drew back, and so saved his neck from the eager fingers of the confessor, but not so his long bands, which were caught and firmly held, so that he was pinned closely to the *grille.*

The noise and confusion caused by this scuffle had attracted the attention of some who had already taken their seats, and a little crowd began to assemble, of faces set to various moods and tones of feeling, some being distorted with half-suppressed laughter, some petrified into a fixed look of alarm, others drawn out into the severest cut of scandalized propriety.

All the time the face of the pinioned priest remained calm and expressive of patient cheerfulness; he neither struggled nor betrayed any emotion.

The captain stood stroking his moustache, and feeling himself a little compromised by the interference of so undignified a champion.

How long the father would have held on to his opponent one cannot say, for the modest step and demure face of the Jesuit put an end to the disgraceful scene. He addressed himself to the priest.

"For shame! my friends, to put our Holy Church to shame in the presence of those not her children. Do me the honour to explain this outrage."

" I will do you the honour to bid you mind your own affairs," cried the confessor, facing round and panting; " this is your doing, and you know it."

" Monsieur le Confesseur, you are at present too angry to judge discreetly of anybody's conduct. I address myself to the priest there."

The worthy priest, having re-arranged his dress, bowed and replied—

" I was humbly doing my duty, and keeping the door of the chapel against that heretic there, and I was assaulted as you saw just now."

" By whose order, may I ask, were you so employed ? " said the Jesuit.

" By your own order, most reverend father," answered the priest simply.

" Alas ! that one momentary act of inattention on your part, brother, should have led to such disastrous consequences. Retire at once ; go back to your chamber in the bishop's lodgings, and repent of your sin. Father Beauvais, and you, M. le Capitaine, will pardon the carelessness of this poor priest, who has not learnt the first lesson of obedience. His instructions were to admit all—Catholics and non-Catholics alike—but, for the sake of order, and in strict justice, to admit Catholics to seats near the chancel, and to reserve the west-end for the so-called Reformed. Was it not so, M. le Prêtre?"

"On consideration, I humbly admit it was; but——"

"Ah! Satan sends that little word 'but' to excuse our sins. Go, brother; he who cannot obey is not fit to rule."

The priest went away, with his large beaver hat under his arm, very crest-fallen; the iron gates were flung wide open, and order was restored.

"That little man will be a cardinal some fine day," whispered Constant to Pierre.

"Probably," answered Pierre; "he has as many bolt-holes as a rabbit."

"Hush! Here comes the procession, and Monseigneur l'Évêque with his crosier."

As the two servants knelt at the stones, Pierre muttered low—

"Please God all bishops and popes may be swept clean away—aye, and kings, too, and kings' women."

The murmured words were not lost upon a monk who paced demurely in the procession.

A face pitted with small-pox turned upon the kneeling *serviteur*, and when Pierre rose to his feet again he knew that the Benedictine had marked him as his own.

Whilst the service of the mass was proceeding in the chapel, Beretti was holding a private conversation with the Comte de Pontorson in the sieur's studio—a conversation 'ad majorem Dei gloriam.' The studio was a small square chamber, wainscoated with black oak; the ceiling had once been gilded and adorned with paintings worthy of a Le Brun or a Mignard, but cobwebs and dirt and damp had defaced the angels, and left a scattering of superfluous wings and purple robes to mock the fancy. In fact, the studio had formerly been a part of the large salon, with which it now communicated by a door concealed behind a bookcase. The walls of this room were hung with book-stands, or adorned with oaken brackets, bearing busts and statuettes of men famous in literature; here and there were suspended rusty rapiers, and antique helmets, foils, fowling-pieces, and stuffed wild birds. The chamber seemed to be a museum of the tastes of the Cornelli family;—the weapons of physical force, old and rusty, pointed to Messieurs les

Ancêtres ; the weapons of intellectual force, fresh from the printer or newly thumbed, betrayed the tendencies of the present lord of the château.

The comte had just thrown himself into a large and comfortable *fauteuil*, square, like all the good arm-chairs of old—a cup of red wine stood untasted by his side ; Beretti was leaning carelessly against the mantelpiece. Pointing to the silver goblet, the latter said, with a playful shake of the head—

" We all have at least one enemy who conquers us, and that red liquor, M. le Comte, is yours. Ha ! ha ! my friend! our order can speak to the point, you see. Stay ! touch not a drop till we have argued this out once for all."

The comte, who had nervously clutched the cup to hide his confusion, now released it at the bidding of the Jesuit, and sat silent, half-supercilious, half-afraid.

" I wish to talk to you," continued the Jesuit, " as one friend talks to another, about this indecent and unmanly habit of yours, which degrades you in the eyes of all when drink has robbed you of your senses. Nay, start not, sir ; I care not if you strike me down with that gay sword that swings so jauntily at your side. I may not bear arms, or I would make mine, too,

leap from the scabbard and satisfy your honour ;
but I am unarmed, and monsieur is no coward,
though he be a ruffling drunkard—— "

" Now, by St. Peter, I can't tolerate this ! "
shouted the comte, starting up and seizing the
Jesuit by the arm.

The Jesuit made no resistance, but when his
arm was released calmly took up the comte's
goblet—" A votre santé, monsieur," drained it to
the last drop, and resumed the conversation
with perfect good-breeding.

The comte's anger was turned to astonishment, and astonishment gave place to admiration, and admiration again yielded to a sense of
absurdity; he threw himself back in his chair
and laughed long and loud.

" There ! that's what I call having a good
heart," said Beretti, smacking his lips ; " another
man would have nursed resentment against me
for speaking so plainly and for drinking his
Bordeaux ; but the Comte de Pontorson has
a good heart, which he is doing his best to
spoil."

" I confess, I confess ; I make a clean breast
of it ! "

" Oh ! that you will never do so long as you
keep defiling it with the fumes of wine."

"Well, well, father, grant me absolution! I am a weak child."

"So much the more need of obeying a strong guide! Come now! put yourself entirely in my hands for six months—I promise you will not repent it."

"No, no! six months on bread and water! Why, I should not be able to drink a cup of cider after that without growing heady."

"Oh, don't boast of your powers of drinking to me, M. le Comte; I have no opinion of your drinking-powers at all. In fact, I am ready to wager a bag of angels that I can sit you out by a good half dozen cups."

The comte gave a look of good-natured, foolish admiration, and ejaculated—

"No! What you—a priest—drink more than I can? Mon Dieu! non!"

"I am ready to challenge you at a drinking-bout; and let this be the condition: that an umpire shall stand by with a hunting-whip, to deliver it to the one who shall remain sober, who shall proceed to scourge soundly his drunken rival; or if both be inebriated, that the umpire shall incontinently punish them both. What say you?"

The comte, restored to good-humour, laughingly refused the challenge.

"Well, then," resumed the Jesuit, "since you strike your colours to me when I challenge you on your own ground, and thereby acknowledge that my head is stronger than yours, ought you not, in mere prudence, to listen to what I have to say?"

"To listen, my friend, is easy; to obey is not always easy or agreeable."

"There you mistake me; that is what you short-sighted mortals always say: 'vice is so entertaining, virtue so uninteresting.' Nothing more untrue. Galloping is exhilarating, walking is tedious; yet you don't put your hunter at his full speed over a heavy piece of plough-land: no, you remember that the chase is yet to come, and you reserve his strength. Now, my good friend, apply this to your own case: your life is but beginning, your prospects are bright, if you can stay the whole course; but if you go on exhausting your powers at the present rate, it will soon come to the last office and a long good-bye, or health will fail and you will find that you have been purchasing a short-lived pleasure at the expense of years of suffering. Just think of this, my friend, that, being sober, you become a rich and noble life, pregnant of good and usefulness; being a drunkard, you become a festering mass of aristocratic corruption, worth nothing, not even the gold braid your cloak is trimmed with. Choose, then, which you will be!"

" Bon Dieu!" exclaimed the comte, rubbing his eyes and starting to his feet, as he shook himself like a dog that has been rolling in the hay; "it has never been put like that to me. I declare you make my flesh creep! What would you have me do? how can I save myself from myself?"

The Jesuit paused, fixed his dark eye steadily on his yielding pupil, and said, in measured words of deep and solemn cadence:

"Go ask the hand of Marie de Cornelli before set of sun!"

The comte looked up, sighed, smiled, stroked his moustache, in every feature and gesture exhibited all the symptoms of in-door relief: virtue, after all, was not so repulsive; vice, after all, was a mistake. The Jesuit went on—

"Affiance yourself to that lady while good motives influence your heart. She is pretty; but shut your eyes to that: you must wed her from higher motives. She is clever and amiable; but what of that? You will become her husband in order to do the will of Christ and his Spouse,

the Church.   I have watched you both carefully ;
you will have a great and good influence on
each other's characters ; you will be happy in
this world ; you will have lived, I have reason to
hope, a good and useful life ; you will have your
reward hereafter."

The Jesuit ended by raising his crucifix to
his lips and murmuring a prayer. He left the
room.   The comte was tracing out a seam in
the old oak floor with the toe of his left boot ;
he was so intent on his occupation, or so taken
up with his thoughts, that he did not observe
that he was left alone.   For several minutes he
remained deep in contemplation of the aforesaid
seam in the floor, then exclaimed, with a sigh—

"But suppose, my good friend, that Marie
should refuse me !"

He looked up for a reply, and found, to his
confusion, that Madame de Cornelli was entering
the studio, her missal in her hand.

Both blushed, both tried to look unconscious,
both read each other's secret.   There was an
awkward pause, then madame said, with a be-
witching smile—

" I thought I heard you talking to some one ;
it seems I was mistaken."

" I—I was talking to myself," stammered the

comte, confused, and playing with the points of his doublet. After a moment's hesitation, he went on, " To tell you the truth, my dear madame, I have some thoughts on my mind which I should like to have the honour of conveying to you."

Madame put a little white hand to her lips to hide a smile that would struggle into notice, and coughed slightly. At the same time she made a mental note of this extraordinary answer to prayer, as prompt as it was literal, for, thought she to herself, " the very thing I have been pleading for the last half hour—the most extraordinary and direct answer I have ever known ! "

" Yes, my dear madame, the good Father Beretti has been taking me severely to task for my irreligious life, and in doing so struck upon a chord which a—which, in fact, had been vibrating for some time in my heart."

" Indeed ! how very singular ! " exclaimed madame, in a suppressed utterance of delight.

" It is so, I assure you ! I should be glad to hear your opinion about it."

" About what ? " cried madame, in a tone of well-feigned surprise.

" Oh, to be sure, I think I forgot to mention

the matter in question. In short, my dear madame, I have the honour to——" The comte paused and coughed, evidently looking for some sign of encouragement.

"Yes?" said the lady, in her sweetest questioning voice.

"To propose for the hand of Mademoiselle Marie," concluded the lover, making his hostess a ceremonious bow.

"I declare you take me quite by surprise, monsieur!" cried madame, remembering her courtly education; but instantly, as if prompted by some religious regard for truth, added, "though, to be sure, I had remarked how very civil you have been to my daughter; but really, I cannot realize my Marie being anything but a child—it comes so suddenly, you know."

"I am sure, my dear friend, that no one could look at your face and imagine you had a daughter old enough to marry," said the Comte gallantly.

"Oh, fi donc! You must reserve your compliments for Marie. To tell you the truth, nothing would give me greater pleasure than to feel that my daughter was married to a good Catholic— but can I truthfully say that of you?"

Madame sighed and bent her blue, languishing eyes on the penitent *roué* so tenderly, that in the depth of his repentance he almost felt as if it were equally improving and equally charming to love the mother as the daughter.

"I declare, upon my honour as a gentleman, that in seeking the hand of your daughter, I am led by honourable and, I may add, by religious motives."

"Sans doute! sans doute!" madame exclaimed, astonished at the speedy conversion of her guest, and fearing his words were too good to be true.

"I should only be too happy, if I could feel sure that my proposals were received with content by yourself and my friend, monsieur votre mari."

Madame de Cornelli gave the comte her hand to kiss, and was beginning to assure him that she would do all in her power to forward his suit, when the door opened and Marie herself entered, in her white muslin dress; and, seeing the comte bending down to kiss the hand of her mother, stopped, curtsied, and was about to retire precipitately, when her mother cried out—

"Stay, my darling, I have a few words for you. Bless your sweet face, how young you look to-day! M. le Comte will, I am sure, excuse ceremony, and leave us together awhile. Go, go! you naughty man!"

The comte gave an awkward skip, which threw his peruke awry, and left the studio with more speed than dignity.

Marie did not try to conceal the smile that his absurd figure elicited. Her mother drew her to her side and kissed her forehead, and spoke softly and solemnly about the service she had just attended; told her how she had prayed for her welfare in the life that was yet in store for her; hoped she would begin to look at life more seriously, as a privilege to be used for Christ's sake and His Holy Church, not as a plaything to trifle with for the pleasure of the moment; asked her to think more of others and less of herself, to do nothing without feeling sure that her guardian angel approved it. This and more did the sincere mother pour into the ear of her daughter, until the dark grey eyes glistened with the tears of good resolve, and the red, pouting lips opened to a smile of filial tenderness. The mother clasped her still closer, till the daughter's face rested on the shoulder of the mother, and then she proceeded to unfold the tender secret which was trembling on her lips.

"Marie, dearest, we can do nothing good on this earth unless we love God—we cannot obtain God's blessing unless we love His Church ; and how sweet it is to feel that you are surrendering anything for God's sake, none can tell but they who have experienced it. Now, my sweet, do not be frightened if I bring this suddenly home to you. You can do something for God by wedding with a man who has the power and the influence and the will, if well directed, to do great things for our holy religion."

Marie sobbed. Madame kissed her and continued—

"Yes, Marie, a great career is open before you, if you only have grace to accept it. M. le Comte has——"

"Ah! mamma, I feared it was so ; but indeed I do not love him."

"No, my child, I did not suppose you loved him yet ; all I wish is that you should not make any violent objections to the proposal—there is time enough yet. I do not wish to lose my darling so soon ; but try, my dearest, to love him, for the sake of our Holy Church."

"Indeed! it is very hard, mamma dear ; very, very hard!"

And the poor girl sobbed as if her heart

would break ; but after a time the swelling
bosom grew tranquil, and the lines melted from
her brow, as she looked up and said, with something
of her old defiant air—

"Why, then, does the good God give me
love with one hand and take it away with the
other ?"

"I don't see your meaning quite, ma mignonne,"
whispered the mother.

"I mean this—though, perhaps, I may be
wrong, for I feel very rebellious—the voice of
God in my nature bids me marry the man I
love, but the voice of God in His Church makes
me sacrifice my love."

"Not always, Marie; if a girl loves a good
man, the Church sanctions and blesses that marriage.
But you must not ascribe every feeling,
however natural, to the voice of God; our
nature, you know, is fallen."

"Yes, madame, but if I may be so bold as
to say so, some of us have been mercifully
redeemed and pre-elected to everlasting life."

At the sound of a strange voice, mother and
daughter started with surprise. There stood
Pierre in his scarlet livery, and three-cornered
hat in hand, bowing to the ground, as he uttered
his sententious remark.

"What do you here at this moment?" exclaimed madame.

"Pierre craves pardon of his mistress; he was sent to summon the ladies, for the games are about to commence in the park."

And the old *serviteur* bowed low, turned on his heel, and retired.

The two ladies laughed as they thought how their Catholic discussion had been brought to a sudden and heretical termination.

"Well, Marie, we cannot stay longer now; but all I wish you to remember is, that both your father and myself only desire your happiness—your real and true happiness; and you know where that lies."

And madame sailed out of the room to attend to her guests, having done her best to disabuse her innocent daughter of the charm of natural love. As for Marie, she looked into the old round mirror to see if her eyes were red with weeping, and having paid that tribute to fallen nature, she sighed once more and ran away to join the throng outside.

By this time the gardens were filled with guests, who were promenading along the terraces, sometimes clustering together and sending up peals of laughter, as some *bon-mot*, a little worse than usual, tickled their Norman risibility; lower down, on the green lawn, children were playing at rustic games, while their parents, in holiday attire, sat round in a great circle and clapped their hands with glee almost as childish. Everybody was bent on being gay that morning, in honour of mademoiselle; the old crooked-backed forester footed it right merrily with black-eyed Jeanne from the village, and toothless Nannette cracked a nut every time the fiddler stopped to wet his lips in the cider. But the merriment was greatest and loudest in the maze, where young men and women of eighteen were racing for dear life, or a kiss, to the pole that crowned the summit. There was no thought in all this festive gathering of Catholic or heretic, saved or lost, slave or free; but rich and poor alike were joined merrily together to spend a Norman holiday.

Most of the nobility and gentry, with their wives and daughters, contented themselves with promenading on the high terraces near the château, whence they could look down upon their humbler neighbours, more noisily merrymaking below; but there were exceptions to this, and the buff jerkin of the apprentice, the long black gown and square cap of the physician, the tall lace caps and coloured hoods of the cottier's wives, were enlivened by many a gallant show of lace and ruffles and shoulder-knots and points; and there were not wanting to the prettier peasant girls partners in the country-dance whose short cloaks, broidered with gold and silver, made sad jealousy brood in the hearts of the once-favoured swain.

Amongst these, and moving in their midst with many a kindly word and hospitable wel-come, came the Sieur de Cornelli, leading on his arm his daughter, who had now exchanged her white dress for an embroidered velvet, the train of which swept the tender grass as she walked. The sieur had a look of proud con-tent on his face, and he often glanced aside with unrestrained delight at Marie, as she bent in return to the respectful greetings of the *bour-geois* and peasantry. As they approached a group of children playing with a swing, all at once the game was suspended, and down an avenue of admiring parents trotted two little children, not more than six years old: they paused in front of Marie and made a low curtsey, and handing to her a little parcel, began to address her simultaneously in childish treble, glancing askance at one another for mutual encouragement, and repeating curtseys at intervals—

"Father and mother can never thank your good father enough, my lady, but here we offer unto you a piece of lace, with our best wishes for your happiness, and may you be as fortunate as you are beautiful."

And having finished, breathless, they again exchanged looks—this time of mutual congratulation—and looked smilingly around at all the world.

Marie opened the parcel and exclaimed—

"Oh! how very pretty! What beautiful lace! Is this for me? Please thank Madame Guillebert, and your father, too, for their kind wishes, and let me kiss you both for your pretty speech."

Then the two little girls were duly kissed, and the grateful parents, who had been hiding in the background, were pushed to the front by their good-natured neighbours, and repeated their thanks and good-wishes, not without blushes and confusion on the part of the farmer.

There was a three-cornered hat hovering about on the outskirts of the little crowd, but it and its self-important owner were forcibly conveyed away from the scene of action by a tall Norman lady before the sieur came that way.

"Madame André has more tact than monsieur the tax-collector," said a buxom wife to her spouse. "See! she is taking the fool away, lest he should spoil all by his majestic mummery."

"Ah! we don't want to hear about taxes on a day like this," exclaimed a withered little woman in a black hood.

"Who talks about taxes, mother?" said a tall, gaunt man, with lanthorn jaws. "Have a care, citizens; there are priests about in disguise, and it were better to go home and hang yourself than say a word in dispraise of his most sacred Majesty's most villainous ministers."

"Always excepting the good Colbert," said another voice.

At this moment a tall old man, with long grey hair escaping from under a square black *chapeau*, broke in suddenly—

"My children, you act very unwisely to cluster together—you will attract the attention of the Catholics—and you, Master Mason, ought to have more sense in your head than to utter yourself so unrestrainedly!"

Several hats were taken off to the speaker, with whom all seemed on good terms.

"You are right, Monsieur la Rose ; it is not a day for such gossip," said the widow, "and priests about in disguise, too!"

"It would be hard for anybody to disguise himself from me," said the pasteur, "for I think I know every face hereabouts."

The widow hereupon fell to such a violent fit of sneezing that she was forced to pull her shawl and hood almost over her face, which she did with a wheezy, asthmatic panting piteous to hear.

The mason watched her narrowly, and looking up at the blue sky and spreading out his hands in the sun, said, with an expressive shrug of the shoulders—

"Quel dommage! the warm sun makes yon poor old widow shiver and sneeze like one with the ague."

The old woman hobbled away. The Huguenots exchanged looks—there was a little pantomine of shrugs and elevated eyebrows before the pasteur said, "Who is yon old woman, Master Mason ?"

"Nay," replied the mason waggishly, "your reverence knows all the faces hereabouts ; and it would be hard for a body to disguise himself from you!"

"Morbleu!" said the buxom matron, "we have been caught in a trap!"

"Yes," answered the mason, laughing, "by an old woman with a tonsure! But I'll see to her shivering fits; I'll follow her ladyship about, and if need be, pluck the petticoats from her false sides!"

"I prythee raise no stir, Master Mason, for the sieur would not for ten thousand crowns that any ill-blood should rise to-day," said the pasteur.

"See, mes amis!" cried the buxom matron, whose sharp eyes had been following the retreating figure of the supposed widow; "the widow is using a kerchief!"

"Bon Dieu!" exclaimed all, turning round; and the pasteur added—

"Then is there no doubt that the old woman is not what she pretends to be; for who ever heard of a poor body having a pocket-handkerchief?"

"And she comes from Paris, as true as I'm a Norman woman," cried the matron, "for there, I am told, the bourgeois are aping the fashions of the gentry."

" Probably yes, madame," answered the pasteur, gravely stroking his chin.

" Then who should it be but one of those Jesuits whom Père la Chaise has sent down to set our teeth on edge ? " cried the matron, triumphantly screwing up her pretty red lips and spitting on the grass.

At this moment the great bell of the château began to ring, and the fiddler paused and looked at the first couple in the country-dance, and the first couple turned and bowed to the fiddler ; and then all the men uncovered to their partners, and all the partners set and curtseyed to the men, and arms were gallantly proffered and coquettishly accepted ; and a slow, decorous movement was made to the great dining-hall, a movement which gradually seemed to quicken and become faster and faster, from a secret feeling of competition for the best places amongst the frolicsome, until it ended in a general run, amid much tittering and falling down of the fair sex.

Tables were spread in both the outer and large dining-halls, and yet many who had come up late were obliged to wait until the rest had finished before they could find seats. Dinner in those days began with meats and ended with soup, and even in the seventeenth century French cookery was famous, and to have a French cook was in England considered a rare luxury.

There was a select party of the nobility and landed proprietors seated at the table which was upon the daïs at the further end of the hall, and behind every lady stood her page or lackey, dressed in a long coat with velvet collar, and glancing down at the undistinguished mob of guests with an ineffable scorn.

The wines of Provence and Bordeaux and Languedoc sparkled beside the native cider, and toothless old dames might have been seen taking very kindly to a silver mug of steaming sack and sugar, or hot canary.

After the Bishop of Coutances had pronounced a benediction, and nimble fingers had made the triple sign of the cross, it needed no pressing to induce the sieur's hungry guests to do justice to the capons and the boar's head and the pork, roast and boiled. But at the lower end of the hall the daintiest dish was the black pudding and the pork sausage garnished with onions, and loud were the commendations bestowed on the authorities in the kitchen.

Amongst the upper guests, Father Beauvais was, as usual, very conspicuous; at his side sat

Captain Guillot, an old friend after the flesh, if not after the Church.

"Ah!" said Father Beauvais, as a dish of truffles was set before them, "you get nothing like this in a Protestant country! Depend upon it, my dear sir, the Holy Catholic Church is the great mother of the cuisine! Then, think of the beneficial effects of judicious fasting, which, apart·from spiritual benefits (which are considerable), imparts such a tone to the stomach. Ah, my dear sir, you Huguenots do vastly err!"

"I shall not venture upon such slippery ground as theology with a father of the Church," said the old captain, smiling good-humouredly, "even though the argument turn upon the respective merits of Catholic and Protestant cookery."

The Abbé Huet, who had been listening to the conversation across the table, now began to rally the ecclesiastical gourmand in a loud voice—

"It used to be the good old custom for our saints, when they met a fellow-creature possessed, to cast out his devil; but it hath been reserved for Father Beauvais to discover a more agreeable remedy; he plies his satanic majesty with *entremets* and fricasseed wing-bone, and so heaps coals of fire on his head!"

"If our friend the good abbé talks less of dainty dishes, it is only because he enjoys them the more—there is no feeder like your closet-student," retorted Father Beauvais, as he wiped the gravy from his moustache.

The abbé burst into a loud laugh at the boyish indignation of the stout confessor, which attracted to him the gaze of the other guests.

"Who is that unpolished little priest?" said a languishing countess to the Sieur de Cornelli, eyeing him through a crystal set in ivory, which she held daintily between her finger and thumb.

"That, madame, is the celebrated Abbé Huet, instructor of the Dauphin, editor of the classics, author of several treatises on theology and philosophy—somewhat rude and impetuous, but a *bel esprit*, and rising genius."

"Humph!" said the countess; "he has the manners of an Englishman!"

The abbé, all unconscious of the disparaging remarks that were being passed upon him, was keeping the company in a roar of laughter.

"You were speaking of my closet studies!" he cried; "I can tell you a story about that. When I was first appointed to the Abbey of

Aulnay, I used to spend a good deal of time at work in my studio, and one day a fellow who was continually pestering my servants to let him in, on being told that he could not see me, as I was busily engaged within, reading, exclaimed, in a discontented tone, 'Diable! why has not the king sent us an abbé who has completed his studies?' Now, my good friend Beauvais, you were the man for Aulnay—I wonder at the king's indiscretion."

CHAPTER V.

BEFORE the guests left the dinner-table, the
Sieur de Cornelli rose up in his place; Constant
stepped forward, glass in hand, to the steps of
the daïs, and shouted at the top of his voice,
"Silence, messieurs et mesdames." Then he
delivered the gold cup to the sieur, who, raising
it above his head, and drawing his sword in his
right hand, said, in the midst of a profound
silence, " My friends, before we leave the table
I give you the health of the king." In an
instant the whole company rose to their feet,
swords flashed in the air, and cries of "Le Roi!"
rent the air, as the red wine disappeared down
loyal throats.

Then the sieur led the way with the Duchess
d'Elbœuf, and the others followed in the order
of precedence. Some of the fine ladies, who
had the air of having been to court, began to

fasten black-velvet masks over their faces, lest the air outside should mar the delicate bloom of their complexions, but the greater part retired to the spacious saloons, where they rested themselves in preparation for the ball which was to take place in the evening. Some gathered round the harpsichord, where Ethel was entertaining them with the English airs that she loved so well; others played at tables, as backgammon was then called, or chess; for the gentlemen there were billiard-tables and smoking-saloons, piquet, ombre, basset, and lansquenet, and red-liveried servants were continually reappearing with confitures for the ladies and muscadine for the men.

Whilst the tournament and mimic contest of knights is progressing in the park, amid loud cries of "V'là!" and "Brava!" let us see what is going on in the private apartment reserved for Monseigneur l'Évêque de Coutances.

He is seated in an arm-chair by the table; before him are spread some manuscripts, which he is deciphering; a white cat is purring about the table, sometimes rubbing her back against the bishop's arm as he leans on the table, sometimes turning brusquely and brushing his very face with her long, furry tail. "Shame on thee,

Candide, thou irreverent creature! thou shouldst have stayed at home had I known thou wouldst be so troublesome—but hark! here comes a mouse!"

And, sure enough, there was a scratching heard at the door, then a pause, then another scratching. "Bien curieux!" exclaimed the bishop, rising and going to open the door. As for puss, she had jumped upon the mantelpiece, arching her back in evident alarm.

On opening the door, Maintenon was discovered with a letter in his mouth, and the sound of retreating steps was faintly audible along the corridor. Maintenon followed the bishop into the room, and seemed in no hurry to deliver his letter, which he held firmly between his clenched teeth, in spite of coaxing and pulling. At last the bishop, not without an angry remonstrance from his canine friend, tore a piece of the paper, and read in the handwriting of Marie, the words, " faire une visite," and conjecturing that his fair disciple sought an interview, he scribbled a large " Oui!" on the remains of the letter, and told the dog to go seek his mistress. This Maintenon seemed to understand, and with one look of ineffable disdain at Candide, who was spitting, like no

Christian, from her ground of vantage, trotted away with his answer.

In a few minutes Marie was kneeling at the side of her bishop, covering his hand with kisses, and trying to repress the tears which would drop, and tell him too soon how sorely she needed comfort.

" Weep on, weep on, my poor little daughter : tears are the precious springs which run to swell the great river of our Father's ocean of love ; there is no human heart torn by anguish, but some angel comforter hovers near to gather up the tears into His bosom. Something vexes my little Marie on her fête-day, and she has come to ask for advice—is it not so ? "

And the bishop parted the hair—the brown wavy hair—from her white forehead, and waited for her confession. Long she knelt sobbing ; at last she ventured to look up, and, gathering confidence from the soft, sympathetic eye which was fixed upon her, she began to narrate, with occasional sobs and heavings of the bosom, the events of the morning, the conversations she had had with her mother, and her own unhappiness at the thought of marrying the Comte de Pontorson, ending by asking, in appealing tones—

"Ought I, then, to marry this man ? Is it my bounden duty, monseigneur ?"

The bishop had a *soupçon* of a smile upon his lips, a glimmer of a twinkle in his eye, as he looked at the kneeling girl and heard the cause of her trouble; he bent down and kissed her forehead, and said—

"Fortunately we shall not need to call in our friends the casuists to settle these doubts of my little one's; no, my dear Marie, it is not your duty to marry that man, and God forbid it ever should be! Your good mother, in her zeal for the Church, has made a pardonable mistake; but, after all, it is your own heart you must consult, for you are a good, sensible girl, and will never give your affections, I feel sure, to one who does not deserve them. Take my advice, and be in no hurry to betroth yourself; especially, Marie, beware of engaging yourself to a Huguenot. Ah! you colour! then I guess aright—do be on your guard, for we know not what troublous days may be in store for us all."

The bishop looked unconsciously at a packet of papers he had that morning received from Paris.

"Now go, and be gay of heart once more, and when any one asks you to wed, fall on your knees and ask the Great Father to show if it be His will—the Spirit will guide you aright— go! you are free!"

Marie left the bishop's sanctum with a lighter heart; the cloud which was menacing her had broken, and above her head the sky was blue. What cared she—a French girl, and only seventeen—for the ominous dark line that stretched across her horizon? She sang a *chansonnette* as she tripped along the corridor.

Meanwhile there had been another dialogue going on in the sieur's studio, in which Marie was no less interested. Lieutenant Henri Guillot, of his Majesty's royal navy, has just been declaring his attachment to the sieur's daughter, and asking permission to win, if possible, the young lady's consent. The sieur stands, for a moment, thoughtful and embarrassed; then, placing his hand on the young man's shoulder, says—

"Henri, I thank you for the honour you have done me in asking my daughter's hand; for, though my rank is above yours, I believe you to be the stuff that nobility is made of—and personal nobility, in my mind, ranks far above hereditary nobility; therefore, I say, I thank you for the honour you have done me. But, *mon cher*, I should prefer to wait a few years before my daughter is affianced, even if she should prefer you—and I have no reason for thinking she would."

The lieutenant winced and hung his head; the sieur continued, in a kinder tone than before—

" Yet, if you like to speak to Marie and sound her feelings, I have no objection ; only let it be clearly understood that there is to be no formal betrothal. There are many reasons for this ; amongst others, her mother is very anxious that she should wed with a Papist : and again, I myself am not quite sure of the advisability of her marrying one of our religion."

" As for the matter of that," replied Henri, twirling his moustache, " I am not so bigoted a Huguenot as to prefer Calvin to Mademoiselle Marie; one religion is in my opinion as good as another."

" That is the worst thing I ever heard you say," rejoined the sieur sternly.

" At my age, monseigneur, you were, I think, of my opinion. It seems to me that the grand religious truths—or rather, the spirit of religion —dominates the heart of youth; one grows older, and a certain set of theological opinions

is imprinted on the mind—the more theology,
the less religion."

The sieur smiled sarcastically and rejoined—

"Rather curious theories for a man to hold
who is willing to become a Papist that he may
marry a Papist! I always thought, until now,
that a Catholic was the slave of certain theological opinions. You, who have no theology,
are willing to enter a Church which will insist on
your accepting every letter of its theological
teaching. It seems to me that it would be more
candid if you were to say : ' I, who believe in
nothing, am quite ready to pretend to believe in
anything to humour the whims of my weak
brethren, so I may wed your daughter.' Ah,
Henri ! the time will come when you will feel
that liberty of conscience is worth some self-
sacrifice, some fighting for. God will some day
reveal Himself to you, and you will feel then
that you cannot barter away those convictions
for anything under heaven. You will scorn to
accept the convictions of other men at second-
hand as your own, when you feel the divine impulse guiding you into truth. The Bible, and the
Spirit given to every man to interpret it—that,
to my mind, is the foundation of religious truth.
No doubt, we shall have a want of unity amongst

us—nay, aberrations and mistaken interpretations, as men confound their own conceits with the teaching of the Spirit; but a live dog is better than a dead man, and a religious conviction, distorted though it be, if only it live and fire the heart, is a thousand-fold better than a correct system of theology, apprehended but not felt."

The sieur paused; his face, generally so calm and tranquil, was stirred with emotion, and there was a kindling fire in his eye which communicated itself to the younger man, as he answered, " You have the advantage over me in living a life of leisure, and are perhaps free from many temptations to which we on board ship are subject. I mix with Papists, most of whom are mere infidels or sceptics; the Papists with whom you come in contact only serve to fan the flame of your religious ardour. I must plead that as my excuse for the indifferentism of which you accuse me."

" My dear friend, do not imagine that my life has not its temptations. What! have I no temptation to join the Roman Church, when I know that any day an order may come from the king commanding me to give up my lands—aye, and my children and the wife of my bosom! Are these no temptations ? "

"Le bon Dieu!" said Henri, between his teeth; "if it comes to that, good-bye to France! I, for one, will never serve a king so tyrannical, so abjectly governed by priests and women. There is the Prince of Orange—— "

"Stay!" cried the sieur, pressing his hand to the young man's lips, " I hear some one at the door!" and he hastily stepped towards the door and opened it.

It was the widow whom we noticed in the gardens; she curtseyed and cried—

"God save your worship! I am almost lost in these dark galleries, and would fain find my way out, begging your honour's pardon!"

The sieur politely begged the old lady to follow him. As they entered the large passage leading to the outer hall, Maintenon, who had been sleeping on a mat, rose with a low growl, and on being rebuked by his master, continued growling in a subdued tone of angry expostulation. The sieur bowed, and, showing his humble guest the way, retraced his steps; but the mastiff thought proper to conduct the suspicious-looking widow to the very door, growling and attracting the notice of the servants in the hall.

" "I never knew that dog so ill-tempered," remarked the sieur to Henri, as he re-entered the studio; "he was quite furious with the beldame."

At one corner of the *salon*, away from the guests who were gathered about the harpsichord and guitar, the Abbé Huet was playing a game of draughts with Marie. They were sheltered from observation by a screen of tapestry work, which represented in vivid red the destruction of Sodom, and the easy transformation of Lot's wife into a pillar of white wool.

By the side of the players stood Philippe and Aunt Justine, making noisy comments on each move, and laughing with malicious glee whenever a piece was crowned king. The abbé was far too good for his adversary, and would soon have swept her men from the board had not the mischievous boy come to the rescue of his sister; for the good abbé would turn away and look out of window after each move, and whilst Marie was planning her next point of strategy, would grow absorbed in his wandering thoughts. Philippe once or twice took advantage of the abbé's want of attention to abstract a piece from the board, not without winking at his sister and nudging his aunt, the latter of whom would show the whites of her eyes in pious horror, and shake with worldly laughter at the successful impudence of her pet nephew. As for the abbé, he would turn to the draught-board and recall his scattered thoughts from the song of Ascra only to find that somehow the game was going against him, and with many a "*hein!*" and many a "*tenez donc!*" re-adjusted himself in his chair and played anew. However, the furtive moves were too much for him, and he was being hemmed in, only to fall a voluntary victim, when Henri came into the *salon* and stood by as the last move was completed.

"*Dux femina facti*," said the lieutenant, mindful of his school-days.

"*Viduus pharetra risit Apollo*," said the abbé, looking at Philippe.

"I wonder," said Aunt Justine, "that a priest should use a sacred language like Latin on ordinary—I may say, profane—occasions."

"If you will permit me to make a quip in the language which you hold so sacred, madame, I would say, *non abacus me turbavit sed abactus!*"

"Oh, I shall run away! I am shocked to hear the Romish jargon—there!"

And Aunt Justine waddled away, angry at not understanding the abbé's Latin, and not being quite sure if draughts might not lead to cards, and who knows whether the clatter of pistoles might not follow to draw down the vials of wrath?

The abbé gave up his place to Henri, remarking that he seemed anxious to be the next victim. Marie coloured a little as she replaced her pieces.

For a time Philippe and the abbé stood by watching the game; but when the lieutenant lost two pieces by default, and had three vacant squares in his king's row, they pooh-poohed his tactics with unreserved contempt, and passed on to the next group.

Henri and Marie were left together behind the blue mountains and the white pillar of wool. It was Henri's turn to move. He was not looking at the board; his chin rested on his hand, his eyes dwelt on the delicate pink face opposite, and his lips were parted as if some spell had been upon him. Marie felt by an instinctive sympathy that she was the object of his gaze, but another instinct bade her look up with surprise, and say sharply—

"Méchant! it is your turn. Why do you look at me so?"

"Because I wish, Marie, to read your heart's secret in your fair face."

Marie trembled and murmured, "Go on!—

with the game I mean;" and having stumbled into this ambiguity, she felt the blush creeping down into her bosom.

Henri continued: "I have your father's consent to speak to you, or I would never have presumed so far, for I am well aware how inferior my rank is to yours, and how unworthy are my claims beside those of some who seek thy hand, Marie. I may say 'Marie,' may I not? You were 'Marie' to me, and I 'Henri' to thee, when we were children together."

"Go on, Henri, with the game. It is thy move;" and the timid girl looked anxiously round, as if she feared some one might be listening.

"I must speak whilst I have the opportunity. I do not ask thee to be my affianced wife—I only want to tell thee that I love thee, and none other; that on land or sea, in the ball-room, on the lonely deck, I shall cherish thy sweet image in my heart, and look forward—may I indeed look forward?—to saying more than I dare say to thee to-day. Give me some sign, Marie, that I may in the hour of battle or in the day of death feel thou too lovest me!"

As he spoke, Henri leaned over the table and put his hand softly on the hand of the

hesitating girl. She did not withdraw it. They
sat for a minute or two thus, neither speaking ;
he with eyes feasting on her face, she not
daring to look up or utter a word. The day's
doings seemed like a confused dream. The
solemn service, the capering morris-dancers, the
shocks of desolation and relief given her by her
mother and the bishop, and now the sudden
realization of her girlish fancies, all crowded one
upon another, had excited her and bewildered
her judgment. When at last she looked up
there were tears in her eyes ; but Henri saw
by the soft light which illuminated them enough
to give him hope for the future.

That game was never finished ; and the
twilight surprised the lovers bending still over
the forgotten kings, and whispering sweet
schemes for the conduct of life's deeper game—
visions of the yet-to-be, moves to be made over
the chequered squares of life.

The servants came in with the torches to
ight up the ball-room, and found them still
bending over their game.

Philippe, sent to summon his sister to dress,
or the ball, came upon them with an exclama-
on of boyish impatience—

"Marie ! we are all looking for you.   I

wonder you are not tired to death. How many games have you played, and who has won ? "

The reverie was broken; the pieces were hurried into the box.

" I can't think how you can prefer draughts to tennis, Lieutenant Henri," said Philippe, with a touch of manly scorn in his tone.

The lovers exchanged looks; if Philippe could not tell why, they could. As Marie rose to leave the salon, the lieutenant touched the tips of her fingers with his lips.

Whilst the guests were donning their bravest dresses for the ball, Father Beretti was better employed in his little chamber in the left wing of the château. A lamp was burning on the table; the large crucifix and rosary had been taken off and laid side by side with a gold chronometer, which ticked defiantly and with something of modern self-complacence in the presence of those mute mediæval emblems. The father was writing in a diary a summary of the day's proceedings, and after completing each sentence he read it aloud to himself. There were confessions of impatience and pride and want of faith, which, after writing, he compelled himself to recite to himself, and then knelt down, and no sound was heard in the dimly-lit room but the ticking of the fussy time-piece.

Then the father rose and fastened the clasps of his vellum-bound *diarium*, and replaced it in a chest that stood by the window, and from the same chest drew forth a pair of silver buckles, which he was attaching to his shoes when a low tap was heard at the door.

"Pace tuâ, pater, aliquid tibi colloqui velim," said Brother Francis, peering through the gloom of the chamber.

"Be seated, brother; if there is aught worth my writing down, have the goodness to be brief and to the point, for I must spend the evening in gaiety, as thou knowest. Well! what hast thou heard? or rather, where hast thou been? for I failed to see thee to-day after the dinner-hour."

The monk seated himself, and folding his hands demurely on his chest, which was covered by the heavy folds of his serge habit, began as follows. "I adopted the precaution of a slight disguise, in pursuance of your instructions to gather the general feeling of our people, and I flatter myself that some good will follow from my innocent expedient."

"Stay!" cried Beretti; "the responsibility of

this rests on you. I never advised you to adopt so dangerous an expedient."

The Benedictine grinned, and showed a row of indifferently handsome teeth.

"If the soldiers of an army are to wait for minute instructions from their officers before they parry the coming blow——" and he shrugged his shoulders and pulled the cord tight which encircled his body. "Non, non! with Brother Francis lies the merit and the responsibility of to-day's disguise. I do not seek to shift the danger, if danger there be, from my own shoulders; but to come to the point— *ut ad rem redeamus*—the Huguenots are as sore as ever on the taxation question, and, though they spoke reservedly, I heard enough to convince me that political schemes are quite as much their *rôle* as religious reforms. I heard the king reviled and his ministers cursed; that infidel Colbert is the man they pin their hopes on——"

"Ah! Monsieur l'Évêque has despatches to day from Paris telling of his serious illness— but all in God's good time!" ejaculated Beretti.

"Then I had the good fortune to overhear something extraordinary in the studio of the sieur, for I was dressed——"

"Tell me not how you were dressed, good brother, that I may answer with a good conscience if questioned at any time."

"Well! as I stood near the door of the studio I heard that infidel lieutenant ask the hand of mademoiselle."

"Jamais! and what then? What, by our Lady, was the answer?"

"He was to sound the demoiselle on the subject of marriage, but at present the sieur declines to betroth her, on the ground of madame's repugnance to 'the Religion,' and the present uncertainty of affairs at court."

"Ha! and—tell me quick!—has the young man addressed himself to her yet?"

"Nay, Father Beretti, you must not expect me to be like the foul fiend, in every place at once," replied the Benedictine grinning; "but what I could I did. I managed to get into the salon when the servants lighted the candles, and there I saw the pretty innocents sitting like brood hens over a covey of draughtsmen, in the darkest corner of the chamber; but the sight of our red livery started them off their seat, and I saw no more: but from the way they looked at one another I should say the compact had been signed with the tongue and sealed with the lips."

"Comment! so soon! Look you now: I urged the comte to press his suit instantly, and had he done so, this mischief might have been prevented—for your girls of seventeen are flattered into saying 'yes' by a title. They will say 'no' to the man they really admire, out of coquetry; while they say 'yes' to a nobleman whom they dislike, out of vanity or ambition."

"It may be so," said the monk, spreading out his hands to express utter vacuity on the subject. "It belongs to you and your order to study the hearts of men and women—to know the secrets of the origin and growth of what the world calls 'love;' as for me, I do not profess to understand it."

"It is well!" said the Jesuit drily, and after a few more words the monk left him alone. As he threw his rosary about his neck, Beretti muttered—

"It is a difficult game of chess when some of the pieces won't move where you wish them, and others think they can move themselves! Now there is no help for it—the lieutenant must be removed from the board!"

And the Jesuit entered in his *diarium* a minute of the monk's narration.

CHAPTER VI.

THE salon of Château de l'Esprit was divided into three apartments, connected by arched galleries. The curtains which usually broke the communication between these rooms were now drawn back, and a person standing at one end of the salon could carry his eye to the flambeaux that blazed on the walls of the furthest chamber.

The large room, or ball-room, was festooned with flags and flowers; large mirrors of polished steel set in silver gilt reflected the gay dresses and flashing jewels of the dancers, and the dark, well-polished floor set off to good advantage the white satin shoes that tripped in the French and Spanish dances.

The centre room was devoted chiefly to the refreshing of the exhausted body; a large table was spread on one side of the chamber with confitures and preserved fruits, behind which

were serving three pretty girls dressed in the
fête costume of the country, and attracting the
attention of many a gallant whose pointed shoes
had done little service in the *contredanse*. The
other side of this room was occupied by a
billiard-table, at which a motley group of
cavaliers and high-waisted dames were playing
an unscientific game with some diminutive nine-
pins set in the centre of the table; but in inverse
proportion to the want of science were the
bursts of laughter as some old dame knocked
over one of these figures in her attempt to
cannon. It was in strange contrast to the silent
and majestic steps in the ball-room that these
votaries of the green cloth stamped and shouted
in their merry humour; it was in contrast, too,
to the grave and thoughtful faces that were
bending over whist and lansquenet and chess
in the room beyond—though here, too, the
silence was broken by the chink of the gold
pieces at each turn of fortune. This, the card-
room, as it was called, was larger than the centre
room, and was fitted up with little round tables
or slabs of marble or malachite, while a con-
tinuous cushioned seat ran round the sides, and
a little fountain of scented water bubbled up
near the oriel window at the end.

Two ladies were standing conversing by the fountain—one a languishing countess, fresh from the court, the other a young and beautiful girl, the daughter of the famous painter Mignard. The younger was dipping her handkerchief in the fountain and putting it to her lips; the elder was eyeing her companion with a supercilious look of pity, and at length exclaimed, loud enough for all to hear—

"Ma chère, how can you touch those odious scents! I should faint if you brought them near my nose—I should indeed! I declare, when I first entered the ball-room and found nearly all the men wearing kid gloves perfumed with scents—orange-flowers and jessamine, and the Lord knows what—you might fairly have knocked me down with a feather! It is abominable! and such an old-fashioned custom!—nearly as bad as yon old Chevalier of the Order, who wears diamonds on his vest, and long boots on his antiquated legs—ah! it smacks vastly of the provinces!"

"Alas, madame! we have not all the privilege of the tabouret at court," said Mdlle. Mignard, with a faint satirical tone in her voice; "but here come the Père Beretti and the Abbé Huet, and I shall learn now how courtiers behave and utter themselves."

The two ecclesiastics were so hotly engaged in argument that they did not notice the ladies, but stood on the other side of the fountain, leaning against its marble base.

"It seems the père is rallying the good abbé on his sporting propensities," said the countess, glancing behind her fan; "let us hear the squabble."

"It is a duty we owe to our neighbour, mon cher," said Beretti, "not to do anything which he thinks wrong. Now, a great many people are scandalized when an ecclesiastic follows '*la course ou la chasse*'; therefore——"

"Stop, stop!" cried the abbé; "I deny your major premise altogether, and I think your conclusion most impertinent. What! is the world to stand still, and are notions of right and wrong never to be modified, for fear of offending a weak brother? Why, the old Roman Emperors thought it wrong to be a Christian, and the Jansenists think it wrong to be a Jesuit! Come now! you yourself go to balls, and dancing, you know, seems very scandalous to some of our pious friends; therefore, *da mihi veniam in venando, et ego tibi salutem in saltando.*"

The two ladies clapped their hands with well-feigned admiration, and cried "*Vive la chasse!*" The card-players looked up and smiled at the Roman jingle, and even an old gentleman forgot to play his pawn, and rubbed his chin with a faint sense of amusement. As for the Jesuit, he was not used to playing second fiddle, and made away into the next room, where the Sieur de Cornelli was conversing with a brilliant group of cavaliers, whose lace collars, reaching half way down the back, and the nice adjustment of whose ruffles and points, betokened familiarity with the court.

But as the confessor approached the group, he perceived that the object of their regard and merriment was a middle-aged man dressed in a plain doublet of black velvet, whose points were untied, and who, with folded arms, was gazing vacantly into space. Yet was not his a vacant face; the nose a little upturned and the broad forehead gave signs of acuteness; but, like Socrates in the market-place, he stood absorbed by his own thoughts, whilst the others pointed at him and whispered, and made bets how long he would continue thus. At length he lifted his eyes from the floor, and, gazing somewhat contemptuously upon the dancers, said aloud to himself, " La félicité est dans le goût et non pas dans les choses," and turning round he found the Jesuit at his elbow.

"What! my friend Jean de la Bruyère here! I thought you were at Caen; but no doubt you have come to make some studies for your characters! Do you want the mocking element? Look here!"

And the Jesuit pointed to the group of courtiers, who were just now looking supernaturally grave and utterly oblivious of the two. La Bruyère only pulled his sword half out of its scabbard and let it fall with a loud ring into its place. This, which was done with so comic an air of defiance, set the courtiers off laughing again; one old nobleman especially was convulsed, and shook with his efforts to restrain himself. La Bruyère seized him by both shoulders, and cried in a loud voice, "Les vieux fous sont plus fous que les jeunes."

The sieur, fearing all this might end in a fracas, and that the king's proclamation against duels might be slighted by his guests, stepped forward to appease the philosopher. Nor was this a difficult task. For the upturned nose had a heart attached to it prompt to forgive an injury.

" Mon ami, we were wagering how long you

would remain in that attitude, when you turned upon us with your quotations from my old friend La Rochefoucauld. Gentlemen, let me introduce to you a man of great ability, one whose name will some day be great in literature—the Theophrastus of our age, if I mistake not—if my learned friend will permit me thus far to reveal the secrets of his studies;" and the sieur added in a whisper, "They have no idea who Theophrastus was, never fear."

La Bruyère bowed, and a young chevalier said, in a tone of banter, "I think, monsieur, you and I have met at court."

La Bruyère looked his questioner down from head to foot, and replied in slow, measured language—

" I have never been to court, monsieur, and that you know quite well; but it will surprise you, perhaps, to hear that the king has sent for me to assist in the instruction of the Duc de Bourgogne; and who knows? perhaps I may there have the honour of mocking at you, my little friend."

The conceited young courtier now looked crestfallen, as his friends rallied him on the brusque language which La Bruyère had addressed to him, and there was quite a buzz of small-talk at the news of the good fortune which had befallen the philosopher of Caen, and presently several little place-hunters came up and craved an introduction to the man whom Louis had delighted to honour.

" Poor man ! " said one lady, " his head will be quite turned."

La Bruyère, who overheard her remark, faced her and replied—

" No, madame, flattery is a false coin which has no currency but through our own vanity, and my vanity has received a shock to-night ; for, to be frank, I came here to ridicule these gentlemen and I find that they are ridiculing me ! "

In the ball-room were several alcoves or recesses in which sat the dowagers arrayed in the family diamonds. From these places of vantage sharp glances were cast from time to time at the timid innocents who were pirouetting in the centre of the room, and frequently a toss of the fan or a motion of the eyebrow settled the destiny of a family yet to be. For obedience to parents was in those days very much in vogue, and in the upper classes, at least, it was very common for parents to sway that obedience to the level of their own financial schemes, and trust that love would follow where wealth had adorned the couch. How different those matrons from the mammas of our own day!—they at least were not ashamed to do openly what they did to effect a *mariage de convenance.* Their theory was that a woman's love sprang up after marriage in the form of gratitude for favours received. Our ladies of fashion have no such theory; they protest that it is wrong to marry their daughters for rank or money, and if they sometimes offer a daughter for sale, they think it much if they have the decency to offer no advertisement to the public. This is what we call the progress of civilization !

As the Jesuit passed from group to group, accosting here and there an acquaintance whom he had met in Paris, and keeping as far away from the dance as he could, to save his reputation for spirituality, after what had been said to him by the abbé, an old lady, much bedizened with lace and jewels, and wearing a canopy of feathers on her head, took him aside into the bow of a window, and, after a few preliminary compliments, said as follows—

" I wish very much to consult you. You are so just and yet so kind in your decisions on all cases of conscience. I wish to consult you about my daughter there—that is she, giving her hand to that handsome officer yonder. The fact is, she has been reading some letters of Jacqueline Pascal, and other of the Port Royal sisters, and has got an idea in her head of taking the vows. Now there is a young nobleman in our neighbourhood— why should I make a secret? the Comte de Pontorson—who, I have reason to believe, is ready and willing to form an alliance with my family. Now, father, am I not warranted in disregarding this silly girl's *penchant* for the cloister, accompanied as it is with admiration for Jansenist doctrines?"

" Madame," replied the confessor, in his most solemn tones, "far be it from me, a priest, to counsel you to trifle with the whisperings of the divine conscience. As for the leanings of your daughter to Jansenism, they will be easily set right when once she mixes with the sisters, but give her to a profligate, and you know as well as I do that you risk her happiness here, and hereafter also."

The dowager bit her lip and said hurriedly, " Mais oui, certainement!" and found means to escape from the rebuke she had so unexpectedly provoked.

As she took her seat again, she remarked to a friend, " My dear, I have received a great disappointment—a great shock to my hopes of worldly advancement. I could not have endured it from the lips of an ordinary priest; but Father Beretti looks you through and through with those black eyes of his. I could not grieve his heart—the dear priest looks so good."

Father Beretti had not walked many steps further before he was accosted by a stout gentleman of about fifty years, dressed in all the luxurious extravagance of the day. A blue cloak broidered thickly with gold and silver was thrown over a black velvet doublet adorned with blue ribbons; a collar of point lace was about his neck, and lace sleeves showed themselves at his wrists; a black ribbon suspended round his neck supported the order of St. Michael; his sword hung by a long chain, silver-gilt; and knots of ribbons at his shoulders and elbows fluttered in the wind raised by the passing dancers. He made the Jesuit a low bow.

" Ah, Monsieur de Blainville! I am glad to see you looking so well."

" And I, father, am rejoiced to meet you

here, for I want your spiritual counsel on the following matter;" and he drew the Jesuit aside and whispered—

"You know my cousin, the late maréchal, died a few weeks ago—God rest his soul! Bien! In his will he has bequeathed a pretty estate in Picardy to my younger son, now six years old, on condition that he be brought up in the tenets of the so-called Reformed Faith."

"I see," said the Jesuit, his bright eyes sparkling with interest, "and you wish to know what is right to do under the circumstances?"

"Precisely!" replied the marquis, stooping to bring his ear to the mouth of the Jesuit.

"The case is clear enough: your cousin has left his estate to your son, attaching certain conditions thereto. You wish to know, first, whether it would be right to accept the estate and the conditions; or secondly, whether you may take the estate and avoid the conditions; or thirdly, whether you ought to refuse both estate and conditions thereto attached. Am I right?"

The marquis grunted assent, and pulled nervously at the slashed sleeves of his doublet. The Jesuit's face grew grave, and he resumed, with a solemn air—" Monsieur, there can be no

question about the first alternative : you may
not—you must not—sell your son's immortal
spirit for a parcel of acres ; take that for certain.
Now as to the second : you know, and I know
too, that to accept the estate and to avoid
fulfilling the conditions attached to it is to act
a lie before God—to promise one thing and
perform another."

The Marquis sighed and said, "Could not
something be done by way of bringing up the
youngster in these tenets in such a manner as
to ensure his rejecting them when grown to
ripe manhood ?"

" Fi donc, Monsieur de Blainville ! that would
indeed be to act a hypocritical part for the sake
of worldly gain. The Church cannot sanction
any such action as that. No, my friend, refuse
the bequest—the Church demands of you this
sacrifice. Come ! what say you ? Will you not
resolve to waive all claim on the inheritance for
Christ and our Lady ?"

The marquis, fascinated by the enthusiasm
and affectionate sympathy of the confessor,
hesitated but a moment before he answered—

" Life is very short, father, and I have few
good deeds to help me out of purgatory. Yes, I
relinquish the estates, since you say it is right."

" Écoutez donc, Monsieur le Marquis, I have been putting your faith to the test. It is true that, as a general rule, he who accepts the gift must likewise, in good faith, accept the conditions of the gift; but wisely have the fathers provided that injury and sin shall not be committed by straining the rule and breaking the spirit in which the rule is conceived. Tenez, monsieur, the power to bequeath by will is not given directly by God, but by men living together in society. Now, society is regulated and held together by the Holy Church, and the Church has power to alter and define the laws of society according as she thinks best for the highest interests of men. Now, to bequeath property under conditions known to be baneful to religion is to forfeit all right to the protection of the Church; and accordingly we find it laid down expressly in the best casuists that where conditions are attached to testamentary bequests which endanger religious or moral life, the heir may neglect the same without prejudice to his or her welfare."

The marquis stood open-mouthed for a few seconds, then settled his *perruque*, and, drawing a handkerchief scented with musk across his face, ejaculated—

"Les petits Dieux! then the lad may take it after all! Good father, I owe you a thousand thanks for your courtesy in listening to my story; and, morbleu! I'll owe the little black Virgin in Mont St. Michel a dozen wax candles!"

There was a crush in the room devoted to the refection of the body: everybody was scrambling for spiced sack and creams, regardless of his neighbour's toes, and the ladies were receiving the slender first-fruits of a feast presently to be devoured by the cavaliers, who just now are looking as if the idea of food never entered their head. Marie is standing by the lieutenant, her little glove resting lightly on his sleeve; she has been so happy all the evening, and her transparent complexion is flushed with a delicate under-tint of rose which makes her look more beautiful than usual. It is impossible to move this way or that, so dense the throng which presses them on both sides; so they glance at each other and whisper, and do not find the pressure of the crowd so very inconvenient after all; and everybody is so gay, and the duennas and the privileged old chevaliers look so smilingly upon her, and pay her most outrageous compliments.

"C'est drôle, mais c'est charmant!" she con-
fides to Henri Guillot, who for his part would
give something if that pretty little hand were
laid in his by priest or pasteur. However, he
knows by an indefinable something in the
delicately soft touch of those fingers on his arm
that at present his star is in the ascendant.

A louder laugh than usual caused the lovers
to turn their heads, and they saw several eyes
directed towards them, and the Abbé Huet
cried—

"Is it true, Monsieur Lieutenant, what they
tell us about your commission and le grand
monarque?"

"Yes, I believe so," said Henri, laughing, but
not quite relishing the joke.

"Oh, do tell me, Monsieur l'Abbé," said Marie,
in a pleading voice; for with a woman's quick-
ness she had divined it was something she
ought to know.

Then the abbé, who could not resist a good
story, even if the point of it stuck into his own
dignity, repeated what he had just heard—

"Eh bien, mademoiselle! You must know
that his most Catholic Majesty has been lately
converted from the error of his ways, and his
royal repentance has assumed two forms—one

moral, the other ecclesiastical; in other words, he has resolved to marry Madame de Maintenon, and he intends, by God's assistance and our worthy friends of the Order of Jesus, to extirpate heresy—if monsieur votre père will pardon the term. Accordingly he sent orders that all Huguenot officers should give up their commissions, and the gallant lieutenant there would have slid into a civilian had he not fortunately had a friend at court."

" How very interesting!" cried Marie; "and did the good king relent?"

" There lies the gist of the story, mademoiselle. The king was told that Lieutenant Guillot was no Huguenot at all, and, in fact, was a total disbeliever in the tenets of Calvin."

Marie just squeezed Henri's arm, and looked up at him with a shy approving glance, and thought, " Then religion will not separate us."

" 'In fact,' said his friend, ' Guillot is an atheist!'"

" 'Comment!' said his Majesty smiling. ' Oh, if he be an atheist, it is all well; let the gentleman retain his commission.'"

A roar of laughter greeted the abbé's story, but before it died down Henri heard, or thought he heard, a sob. He looked at Marie; her face was turned from him. Suddenly the great chapel bell tolled for a midnight service, and the crowd began to break up into groups. 'As soon as she could, Marie withdrew her arm from the lieutenant's, and saying in a cold voice, " Excusez-moi, monsieur," glided away.

It was a moment or two before Guillot could realize the full bearing of events. He stood in the centre of the room, stupefied by the sudden catastrophe which had overtaken his heart's dearest joy, feeling that he himself had created the gulf which the learned chatterbox had so thoughtlessly uncovered between himself and her he loved. To prevent any explanations, he had himself owned to the truth of the story.

As he stood biting his moustache, the Jesuit confessor drew near.

" Hélas, mon ami! I need not ask you to accompany us to where the bell is calling us; at present you are young, and in the strength of your youth cannot lfit up your eyes to Him who gave it. I know many a poor bedridden cripple who is happier far than you, my son."

" Indeed you may, for I am most miserable," faltered Guillot.

The priest gave him a sharp look out of eyes that lightened with a strange flash of intelligence, then passed on with measured step and lowered head.

As Beretti entered the chapel, he had thought over some new combinations, and was glad that so important a piece need not be removed from the board.

It was a strange and startling transition from the ball-room to the dimly lit chapel, from the gay music of the paid performers to the deep voices of the priests as they chaunted the evening psalms. Yet madame had prevailed upon the bishop to stay and conclude the fête, as it had commenced, with prayer. There were not many now assembled, but those who knelt to-night were making no compliment to the religious feelings of their hostess; they were Catholics or large-hearted Huguenots, and the vaulted roof re-echoed with heart-felt cries, the aspirations of man's better nature.

The bishop had turned to pronounce the benediction, but first offered a few earnest remarks on the love of Christ which makes us all one family, and asked the prayers of those assembled that Christ would knit together in His love the members of his diocese.

As the last words of the benediction died away, a silence fell on all, broken only by a wayward sob that ever and again seemed to break away from the control of the weeper.

Then the tramp of a horse outside, and a knocking at the chief entrance, and a sound of many voices shouting, clashed upon the ears of the silent worshippers; and when the sieur was passing out of the *grille*, a courier, stained with mud, ran forward, gave him a· packet of papers, and whispered. The sieur turned round gravely to his guests, and said simply, " Colbert est mort !" The words were caught up by the guests in the hall, and with blanched cheek or exulting tone repeated: " Colbert est mort !"

CHAPTER VII.

THE Comte de Pontorson returned to his château the day after the fête, and caused some inconvenience to the old *châtelaine*, who had not expected her lord home so soon. Indeed, it was evident to the page who received his cloak, and the valet who dressed his peruke, that something had gone wrong with their master; and he did nothing but swear and drink by the hour for ten days in succession after returning from the Château de l'Esprit. If he spoke, it was in praise of dogs and in contempt of women, so that la mère Clélie, as the good housewife was called, would shake her head wisely over a cup of sugared Rhenish with the apothecary, and confess to having a shrewd suspicion that Monsieur le Comte had been snubbed by that little *marmouset*, Mademoiselle de Cornelli.

It was too true!—the great financier, the friend of the Huguenots, Colbert, was dead! To his contemporaries only a heavy, beetle-browed man!—one who would spend fourteen hours a day stooping over his desk—a stern, harsh refuser of applicants for comfortable sinecures, unpleasantly honest in all his dealings, and consummately indifferent to the squabbles of Jesuit or Jansenist, of Catholic or Huguenot ;— and so the gentle citizens of the gentlest city in the world hooted his remains as they lay in state, and compelled his sorrowing relatives to whisk him off to St. Germains under cover of night! What was it to them that he had created a navy, and made, or tried to make, his country independent of others as far as the necessaries of life were concerned? What recked the bloated minions of Louis le Grand of ·attempts to cheapen food and encourage commerce, arts, and letters ? He is dead! The old man, worn out with toil and saddened by the failure of his dearest hopes, has migrated to another clime, another planet perchance; but he leaves his body behind him, and a fame clouded by prejudice. As the one crumbles to decay, the other will brighten ; but it will needs be that an ungrateful people pass through the fire of affliction before they learn to recognize the value of sincerity, truth, and honesty.

Colbert had supported the Huguenots because they were the best citizens, the best traders, the most industrious and thriving part of the community. Little by little encroachments had been made by royal authority on the sphere of exertion permitted to the Protestants. First, the little shopkeepers, the needlewomen, the laundresses, had the means of procuring a living reft from them; then the interdict rose higher in the scale of professions, and merchants, officers, magistrates, were compelled to abjure or forfeit their positions. And when honest old Colbert was drawn away at a hand-gallop through the dusky streets to his last resting-place, there was no one left strong enough or brave enough to plead for the persecuted; no, not even to say, "They are useful to us—they are well-to-do and can pay the king's taxes; let them alone."

The summer months came and went as usual, the sun shone just as fiercely on the backs of the Reformed as on the best of Catholics, the green trees did not refuse their shade to them, and the birds sang to them in the branches; but their Norman neighbours began to look askant at them; the priest when he met them would cross the road to avoid them ; if they were sick, they must not call in the pasteur; if they chose to die, they must get themselves buried before six o'clock in the morning, or, if they prefer it, after six in the evening—and woe be to the mourner who shall presume to offer up a prayer aloud ! When they sing their psalms in their temples they must stop suddenly, even in the middle of a canticle, should the Host pass by outside ; if their temples are built in the vicinity of a church the mob may burn them to the ground. Should there be any scoundrels amongst them ready and willing to forswear their faith for a trifle, the generous Pelisson will reward them at the price of six livres per convert ; and, to prevent any mistakes, the converted shall have given him a certificate, duly made out and signed by the authorities upon the back of the knave of spades or the king of clubs, as the case may be —and it shall be known amongst the Reformed as " the mark of the beast."

Such grows to be the condition of affairs at Coutances shortly after Marie's fête. The Comte de Pontorson comes no more to the château, for he has pressed his suit to little purpose, and, like a spoilt boy crying for what he cannot have, he is sulkily sipping his life away. The Jesuit was not invited to prolong his visit, and so he took a lodging with his sacred *confrères* near the cathedral, much to the excellent bishop's dismay, whose Gallican tendencies were leading him further and further out of sympathy with the policy of the Order of Jesus. There, however, he had installed himself, like a cat watching a lion, and the pitted cheeks of the Benedictine were a familiar object to the *gamins* of the streets of Coutances.

Madame de Cornelli came as usual at stated times to worship at the altars and present trinkets and wax-candles to the Virgin; and not unfrequently when she whispered her shortcomings in the confessional, it was Father Beretti who apportioned her penance.

Lieutenant Henri had never seen Marie again since she left him so brusquely in the ball-room; but as old Pierre drove him in madame's glass-coach to Avranches, he handed him a billet sealed with wax and tied with tape, which billet the lieutenant opened when he saw that his father was comfortably asleep in a corner of the coach, and which ran as follows :—

"HENRI,

"Forgive me if I seem to you to judge rashly, but I owe it to my father and good mother, as well as to myself, to tell you at once, before it has become irreparable, that there are reasons why you and I can never marry, and why, if we did marry, we could never be happy. Think kindly of me, Henri; and, oh! if you knew what pain it gives my wicked heart to pen these few lines, you would appreciate the motive which prompts them. Adieu!

"MARIE."

The young man kissed the blurred lines reverently, and placed the letter of dismissal as tenderly in his breast as if it promised him his heart's desire. Such is youth!—strong and hopeful and trusting!—and who can say to youth, "Try not; it is impossible"?

It was now the summer of 1685. The little town of Coutances had been gay with ribbons and banners, and processions of priests had paraded the streets all the morning, with their usual appendage of gaping women and squalling babes; but the hot afternoon had cleared the open spaces of loungers—nothing stirred in

the glaring sunshine but an occasional cat, and
the flags drooped lazily from the gable ends
of the houses. You would have said that all
Coutances was asleep had not yonder side-
door in the old cathedral kept up an inter-
mittent creaking, as old women hobbled in or
hobbled out. Is it because the air is so
deliciously cool here that vespers have drawn
so goodly a show of worshippers? or have the
country people flocked into the town to see the
fine doings this holy day? See! beyond those
iron gates which separate the chancel from the
choir are faces familiar to us two years ago.
There sits the little secretary, very demurely
perusing his Paternoster, as if it were entirely
new to him and it needed all his attention
to decipher it; there is the clear-cut profile
of Monsieur l'Évêque, a striking contrast to
Father Beauvais, who sits opposite to him;
there too are Beretti and Brother Francis, and
a dozen more, mostly with withered faces and
decrepid frames, or labouring under a mountain
of too-solid flesh.

And here, amongst the throng of women who
cluster by the *grille*, are two faces we recognize.
The younger has her eyes fixed upon the dark,
melancholy face in front of her; but it is not

the mitre which attracts her gaze. A young woman's religion is almost always personal, and Marie de Cornelli has many chords in the diapason of her being which strike in harmony with her bishop. But she glances aside every now and then with a look of anxiety at the pale face of her who sits beside her—she places her a footstool, and tenders her the phial of salts and vinegar.

The toothless goodies who notice these attentions on the part of Marie drop their beads and whisper together, nodding their wise heads and shrugging their surprised shoulders. The intelligence passes quickly down the nave to the old beggar woman who sits clinking two sous in a tin box at the western door. One would think it was a part of the evening service, so decorously is the news passed from one row of chairs to another.

What news? So said the old men, who sat on the other side of the cathedral, and could not for the life of them make out what all the gossips were making such a fuss about.

As for Madame de Cornelli, the tears were blinding her eyes too much for her to see the interest which she had evoked in the feminine portion of this inquisitive little country town.

When the good fathers had got through their vespers, and the last fat priest had disappeared into the *vestiarium*, and the old oak door was creaking and banging to the exit of humble worshippers, Madame de Cornelli, folding her black lace veil closely over her face, walked slowly to the south aisle of the cathedral, and entered one of the confessionals. Marie was joined by a handsome blue-eyed boy of about fourteen, whose black velvet doublet, relieved by a narrow collar of lace, threw into relief a clear pink and white complexion. To compare the complexions of the two was to see at once that they were brother and sister, though in other respects their faces presented few points of similarity : the blue eyes and straight nose of the boy were in full contrast to the dark grey eyes, black eye-lashes, and slightly upturned nose of his sister. When we saw them last he was but a child; two years have put more than the same number of inches to his stature, and Philippe treads the old slabs of the cathedral church with just a touch of conscious self-importance.

The two retired to a corner on the north-west side, and, seating themselves on two chairs, awaited the approach of their mother. Marie took out a little book and began to read. Philippe, in pensive thought, tapped lightly on the pavement with his riding-whip. This continued for some minutes; at length he looked up—

"Ma mie, what is that you are reading so earnestly?"

"Les Fleurs des Saints," replied his sister, dropping the book on her knees.

"I wish, Marie, my mother would not confess to that fellow Beretti! Why can't she be content with Beauvais, I wonder?"

"Father Beretti is a much more cultivated man, you must allow."

"Oh yes, cultivated with a vengeance! He is like our new gardener: he is for cutting off the dead branches before they die, to show his skill and zeal in gardening—all very well for healthy shoots like you and my mother."

"Mon petit frère, speak not so loud, I beseech you. You frighten me when you talk like that. What grounds have you for such ideas?"

"Comment donc! is he not a Jesuit? and are not the Jesuits the spring that moves the king and that Madame Maintenon? and have not Catholics and Huguenots been set by the ears ever since Beretti came down to

Coutances ? and does not ma mère come away weeping from his confessional ? Why, then, does she weep ? "

" Nay, mon frère, I can hardly follow you, so rapid are your questions. But—is that old priest within ear-shot, think you ? "

Philippe turned in the direction indicated, and bending his head, whispered—" Speak low, Marie, and the *chien* will not overhear us."

" Well! I, like you, thought that something was on my mother's mind, and one afternoon as I passed her room I heard her praying aloud. The words came so distinctly to my ear that I could not help hearing, and, indeed, something made me pause and listen. She was sobbing and crying out—' If it be possible, let Thy servant be spared this cup of sorrow, sweet Lord! Ah! tender-hearted Marie! thou hast been a wife and canst feel with me. Plead for me, that I may not be obliged to quit my husband, my dear, sweet heretic! Ah! if it be possible!' Such and more la pauvre bonne mére ejaculated, and a great knot mounted in my throat, Phil, and I ran away with oh! such wicked thoughts in my heart!"

The brother looked very grave for some minutes, sighed, and said—

" Then it is as I thought. I must tell my father ; it will decide him to leave the old place, I fear—*la belle Normandie*, and all the dear associations of home. Oh, Marie, you should have told me this before! That wily Jesuit wants our mother to go into a convent, *sans doute;* then he will push my father into open conflict with the clergy, and, of course, the hare will either leave her form for the pursuers or will be eaten up skin and bone."

" I can't think it right of the confessor to give such counsel," said Marie ; " if indeed it be he who so advises my mother."

" Çà-mon, ma foi! surely you cannot find fault with it, since you did the very same thing yourself when you threw off Henri."

The colour mounted into Marie's cheeks, and a tear sparkled on the dark lashes that fringed her eyes, as she replied—

" God knows, I did it for the best. It was a hard struggle of conscience against heart, as you know. I loved him then ; I thought he loved me ; but all that is changed now. He forgot me sooner even than I had—than I had expected. He left the king's service, and never said 'adieu' to my father, who loved him so well. Was I not right in refusing his hand, mon cher ? "

" I was too young to notice much at the time, but I remember the passionate way he took me up in his arms the next morning, when he was starting for Avranches, kissed me on both cheeks, forehead and mouth, and in his confusion murmured, ' Adieu, Marie ! ' "

The tears were falling stealthily on the pavement.   Marie put up her hand and adjusted a demi-mask of black velvet, which she sometimes wore out of doors, and which concealed the brow and eyes.

Philippe drew a miniature portrait, set in pearls, from his bosom.   " This was sent to me a few days after he left by Henri—it is his mother's likeness.   I never received it ; but this morning, as I was ransacking one of my mother's drawers, I found it wrapped in a piece of paper and addressed to me.   I took it up, and found a few words scrawled here on the back—' To the one who loves me best.'   Will you take it, Marie ?   It is a curious old portrait."

Perhaps the young lady did not notice the slight tone of raillery in which Philippe's words were uttered.   She answered calmly—

" Give it me, mon mignon ; it is his mother's portrait—he valued it above all other possessions. You had better let me keep it—for a time."

And so the grand old lady in her pearl border once more changed hands. Marie held it in her hand and gazed upon it till the tears blinded her and she could no longer distinguish the lineaments of that weather-beaten face. She murmured something of " Papa's dear friend," and kissed it on the score of fond antiquity ; but Philippe was not to be taken in by such wiles as these, and loftily curled the lip of scorn, with all the hauteur of a fourteen-year-old philosopher.

The portrait was hardly consigned to a warm place near Marie's heart when a tall veiled figure approached them. There was something just now rankling in Marie's heart concerning the keeping back of the miniature which made her turn away from her mother with a momentary feeling of dislike. Philippe, on the other hand, pressed his mother's arm tenderly, and said, " We have thought you long to-day, sweet mother ! I fear you have tired yourself, and you have been crying ! Ah ! we must take you to see le bon évêque : he will give you comfort, and not sorrow, like some do."

" Mon cher petit, thank you for your kind sympathy ; thank you, dear boy ! "

And the white hand carried a kerchief to wipe the blinding tears away. The boy's words had gone like arrows to her heart, for her struggle in the confessional had been to learn to surrender him and his father for the greater glory of God; and now this burst of boyish sympathy had made the old wells of natural affection overflow again; but there was no look of sympathy from the daughter, whose religion ought to have drawn her closer to her mother, for whose sake the latter was prepared to sacrifice much that was dear!

As the three passed out of the north-west door the old hag in the corner clinked her sous, and a few *deniers* were added to the store, in return for which she bestowed her blessing on le petit monseigneur et mesdames. As they walked down the narrow street towards the hostel "La France," where Pierre and Maintenon were waiting for them with the *calèche*, they were met suddenly, nearly opposite the Church of St. Nicholas, by a crowd of men, women, and boys, who, with loud shouts and roars of laughter, were tugging at some heavy object which was partly carried and partly dragged along the roadway.

Madame de Cornelli would have fared ill

against so rude a mob, had not a mule which was tethered to a ring in the wall afforded her a moment's shelter. Instinctively she pulled Marie between the mule and the wall, and the surging crowd would have gone by without harm had not the burden which they were carrying slipt from the shoulders of the bearers and fallen just opposite the mule with a metallic clank upon the hard stones. Thereupon arose a fresh burst of merriment, and one little ruffian, recognizing Philippe, cried out, "Ventrebleu! the beast of a Huguenot bell is doing homage to the young lord there. Flog it, mes amis, flog the beast of a bell!"

And accordingly, some with sticks and some with their leathern aprons set to and be-laboured the heretical bell, till the place rang with the echoes of the bell-metal. The most furious blows, however, were those dealt by the women, some of whom had taken off their wooden *sabots* to give the *coup-de-grâce* to the object of their fury ; and the devilish gestures of these termagants were in strange contrast with the gaiety of the boys and men, to whom these proceedings were more of a facetious piece of horse-play than an act of religious retribution.

As the crowd gathered round more densely, and coarse words came to the ears of the Cornelli family, making madame fold her daughter closely to her bosom, as if to shield her eyes and ears from impurity, a square black cap and a red face were thrust out of a window just above them, and a husky voice cried out—

"Would madame please to accept the shelter of an apothecary's poor lodging until the lewd folk disperse ?"

"A thousand thanks, Monsieur l'Apothicaire," cried madame eagerly.

Instantly a little door was opened, and the apothecary in his long black gown stood bowing, and conducted his guests into the best parlour.

"I regret to say that Madame Bienaise is not able to do the honours to my Lady de Cornelli ; that good woman is, pour le moment, engaged with her young baby upstairs, or she would only be too proud. May I——?" and the polite apothecary handed his guests a little tray of confitures heaped about a silver goblet of muscadine, being an attention which he reserved for patients of the highest quality.

Madame declined the proffered gift with a gracious smile, and inquired after the health of Madame Bienaise, adding—

"I was not aware, monsieur, that you were blessed with any children."

"Non, madame, it is but of recent date. My wife and I, we have lived together now these fifteen years, and no little one came to bless our house; but at last we bethought us of a plan—and I wonder it escaped us so long —it was as follows: my wife was to make a pilgrimage to Mont St. Michel; she was to make her vows (and some little offerings, too) to the black Virgin in the chapel there, then she was to return to her husband—c'est moi— and then! why then, madame, she was to wait and see if the black Virgin had deigned to hear our little petition. Voilà! il est accompli enfin!"

"How very interesting! and when was the babe born?" asked madame.

"This morning, madame, as I was eating my omelette; Jésu be praised!"

The two ladies gave little exclamations of surprise, and as the apothecary turned to offer a glass of sack to Philippe, Marie could not resist whispering to her mother, "That good woman is engaged—*pour le moment!*"

Philippe had been gazing out of the narrow window which looked into the street; as the apothecary craved his acceptance of a glass of wine, he turned round and asked him if he knew the meaning of all the uproar going on outside, and why they were dragging about a bell.

"Is it possible!" cried M. Bienaise. "Have not my noble guests heard that an order has come from Paris for the demolition of all the temples in the province? Non! il est vrai maintenant. And the garçons yonder have seized the bell which used to call the Reformed to prayers, and God knows what they mean to do next!"

"And there is old Pierre talking to the lanthorn-jawed mason, and screwing up all his features into one," cried Philippe.

"And see, monseigneur, how quietly my good mule takes it all!"

"Of course, Monsieur l'Apothicaire, your mule is a patient. I doubt not you try on him the potency of your clysters and your soporifics."

"Ah! it is a wise animal that; he never minds other people's business."

"But I have a mind to see the end of this same bell," said Philippe to his mother; "you and Marie are safe here under such excellent protection—I will but join Pierre outside for a short space."

They tried to persuade the boy to remain prudently with them ; but an only son is seldom guided by the advice of a fond mother at the mature age of fourteen, and entreaties only fired his adventurous spirit the more. He saluted the apothecary and went out.

On the top of the bell, which still lay where it had fallen, a little man with a bald head was standing and addressing the crowd in excited and angry tones. At the end of each sentence he paused and looked round for applause, which was given him in a low, subdued murmur of assent. As Philippe approached he was getting out of breath, and some such words as these he uttered with a snappish voice—

"Hé bien, mes amis ! if these things be so— if I have told the truth about these lying, traitorous, atheistical Huguenots," ("Il est vrai !" murmured the crowd) "if they want to pull down the priest from the altar and the king from his throne," ("Les maudits !") "how long, I ask—how long shall these scélérats cumber the ground ?"

"Get down, get down !" cried a fat, burly priest, who was edging his way through the throng.   The rubicund priest was popular, and the crowd shouted " Descendez donc !" to their orator.

But his descent was prematurely balked by the sudden raising of the bell upon the shoulders of the mob, who, with infinite laughter, now watched the funny efforts of the chagrined prophet to preserve his balance upon the wooden frame-work of the bell.

" This is no place for you and me, Monsieur Philippe," said Pierre, as they rubbed shoulders with the fruiterer's errand boy and laundress's apprentice, and followed the crowd up by the cathedral, and away again to the left.

Philippe made no reply, but silently nudged the old *serviteur*, and nodded to the bell which went before.   On they went through the narrow, winding streets, now lying in shadow, as the evening sun inclined to the Gulf of St. Malo ; and as they passed by the stalls of the merchants and the booths of the vendors of sweets and ecclesiastical trinkets, old goodies came out a-gape, or ran within to fetch their wooden *sabots*, in haste to see the sport that was toward.

When at length the procession reached a level space on the outskirts of the town, which was planted with limes and looked towards the east on a sheer fall of some three hundred feet into the valley, and commanded an extensive view over undulating fields and forest—there the bell was deposited ; the little sallow-faced, bald-headed orator was glad to reach *terra firma;* and there was a hush of some seconds while the chief conspirators discussed the next stage in the proceedings. At length a circle was made about "the heretic," and two or three delvers who chanced to be passing at the time were pressed into the service, and exhorted to dig a grave big enough to contain "le monstre." Then some one arrayed himself in the frock and broad black cap of the pasteur, and was proceeding to read a burial service in mock solemn tones, while others, catching at the spirit of the thing, lifted up their voices and wailed in well-counterfeited grief, when the tall form and long white hair of La Rose, the Protestant pasteur, was seen approaching. In-stinctively the circle cleft itself and made way for him to pass through. He went straight up to the chief performer, and, arresting him in his utterances by a pat on the shoulder, proclaimed in a loud voice, with a good-natured twinkle lighting up his fine grey eyes, and the many-circling lines of his face melting into a genial smile—

"Mes enfants, do you not know the law? I must give you fair warning that you are this day making yourselves amenable to the king's officers for breaking his laws concerning the conduct of heretics. Mais oui, mes enfants! What do I see here?—a pasteur reading a burial service in the open air! Messieurs, il est défendu! it must not be!—encore, mes amis, a heretic is about to be buried before six of the clock! Messieurs, il est défendu! it must not be!—encore, mes amis, will you bury a creature before life is extinct? Speak! tell these kind people, Mademoiselle la Cloche, that you will wait three quarters of an hour before you bury yourself!"

And the aged pasteur seized the tongue of the bell and gave four vigorous pulls, making the silent evening clash out into such sudden echoes that the rooks flew cawing about the trees affrighted. There was a great roar of laughter at this unexpected ending of the service, and cries of "Vive La Rose!" rent the air.

The old man replaced his *chapeau*, which he had held in his hand during his appeal to the people, and had some difficulty in answering to all the requests to shake hands which were pressed upon him by the fickle crowd.

"The time is not yet," muttered an ill-looking fellow to his neighbour, as they left the lime-grove in disgust.

"No," replied the other in a foreign accent; "these Frenchmen will be friends with any one who tickles their stomach or their fancy!"

As Philippe stood watching the dispersing crowd, the lean and lanky mason approached him, doffed his cap, and suggested that, in the excited state of the townsfolk, it would be better to conduct madame and mademoiselle home as quickly as possible.

"To be sure!" said Philippe with a consequential air. "You speak with your usual prudence, Maître Durand. But what is this?"

Durand was offering a scrap of paper for acceptance.

"Would Monsieur Philippe be so kind as to bear this to his respected father? It is a request from the elders of the church."

As Philippe and Pierre retraced their steps, the old *serviteur* sang under his breath, "They imagined a mischievous device, which they are not able to perform."

CHAPTER VIII.

THREE days after the events recorded in the
last chapter there was a party of peasant
women and young girls busily engaged in
beating dirty linen with smooth stones from
the brook which runs through the valley at
the foot of Coutances. It was a hot noon-tide,
and the birds, having more leisure than those
who consider themselves their superiors, had
withdrawn to their leafy coverts, whence, in
calm indifference, they blinked their eyes at the
motes which floated between them and the grey
cathedral, or nodded off into the drowsy realms
of Morpheus. But human beings, being so
superior, must wash their dirty linen in sunshine and in shade; and to-day those who can
have spread their sheets and stockings beneath
the willow-trees which fringe the banks of the
purling brook, watched by merry little children,
black-eyed and hollow-cheeked—for food is

passing dear when you have great victories
to pay for. The mothers and the elder sisters
are busy down there below amongst the
boulders and the rushing water, and many a
jest floats on the still air, and many a ringing
laugh is answered by the inquisitive rooks from
their eyrie in the lime-walk opposite.

There is a little wooden bridge over the
brook, and a footpath rises up the steep ac-
clivity on the further side, leading to an out-
lying hamlet. A few paces up this footpath
and you come to a snug little cottage on the
right, garlanded with jessamine and roses,
having in front of it a tiny garden, cultivated
within an inch of its existence, from the end
of which you can look down upon the bubbling
streamlet. There are two children there now,
one a little girl of seven years with deep-set,
lustrous eyes, and another about three years
older ; the younger is seated on a rustic bench,
propped up with an old bolster, the elder
stands by her side, weaving a garland of wild
flowers. From time to time they look over the
hedge and kiss their hands to a nice-looking
woman who is washing apart from the rest, at
a little distance down the stream, unnoticed by
her fellow labourers.

" Would you like to walk about the garden now ? " said Marguerite, the elder, to her young sister Jeannette, who is recovering from rheumatic fever, and half reclined over the back of the seat to watch the process of washing, wringing, and drying, and to encourage her mother with private nods and mystic wavings of emaciated fingers.

" Non, non, Marguerite ; let me be, let me be a while ! See, there is mammy working, working so hard down yonder, and no one helps her, no one speaks kindly to her ; non, ma petite, let me stay here a while—mammy loves to see her pauvre mignonne looking at her. See ! she looks up and smiles ! Ah ! comme je suis heureuse ! "

Marguerite looked wonderingly at her sister. She could not comprehend the infinite delicacy of feeling that kept that poor wasted child gazing there hours together, till la mère returned with the big basket on her head, and the wooden clogs clattered on the sanded floor of the kitchen. It is only sickness that brings out prematurely and ripely the full sympathies of which the heart is capable. The one sister, straight and strong, brown as a berry, needing no sympathy and capable of giving little in return ; the other bent and enfeebled, with cheeks of ashen grey—one who had plucked the flower Love out of the nettle Suffering, a child in mind, a woman full-grown in heart, and thrilling in every fibre in sympathy with her who had smoothed the crumpled pillow, and whispered the prayer of faith in the silent watches of the night ; and now to do what she could to help that patient mother was her only delight. And the dark eyes lit up her colourless face like two lamps as she lisped, " Ah ! comme je suis heureuse ! "

" And now, Marguerite," she said, " go down and help mother wring the linen, for I shall do very well here. I begin to feel so well, now that the sun shines, and my bones don't ache as they used."

Marguerite was glad to avail herself of the opportunity to be away and be doing something active with her brawny limbs. With bare feet and lanky brown legs she sped down the path and across the wooden bridge, and was by her mother's side in an instant. Her mother turned upon her a young face grown old before its time, and with a little bitterness cried—

" I thought I told you not to leave Jeannette ! You are no use at all ; you don't do as you are bid ; you are naughty—go away ! "

The child pouted and dug her great toe
deep in the sand at the bottom of the stream,
making great bubbles float to the surface. The
mother went on with her work, the child
continued her sulky explorations for several
minutes, and neither spoke. At last the brown
face looked up at the hedge, then ventured to
draw near her mother and whisper—

"See, mother, little Jeannette is smiling
at us!"

The mother turned and kissed her hand.
She was no longer angry with Marguerite—the
smile of the little sick child had soothed her
fretting nerves. It was a ray from heaven, and
she seemed to see written up over the fire-place,
in her husband's own writing, the familiar text,
"Blessed are the peacemakers, for they shall
inherit the kingdom of heaven."

Mother and daughter began to work together.
There was a goodly pile to get through before
all was done, for M. Arnaud, the Huguenot
chirurgeon, was about to marry his daughter
this week, and that made "extra washing for
extra pay," as the mother cheerfully observed to
her little girl.

"I'm sure we need not grumble," she added,
"for now the works at the cathedral are shut

against your poor father, it is little enough he
can earn to buy his wife and children bread
and pottage; though, to be sure, he is the
cunningest master-mason in all Coutances, and
Monseigneur l'Évêque himself said that one of
his angels' faces that he carved in the Lady
Chapel was equal to your tip-top masons at
Paris yonder. However, God's will be done!
It is a weary, wicked world! Look alive there,
Marguerite!"

With these reflections the poor laundress
pounded away at M. Arnaud's linen with more
vigour than discretion; and when the good
chirurgeon again settled his cravat and pulled
out his full sleeves, he might have noticed with
small satisfaction sundry tiny indications of
schism.

We left the little Jeannette in the garden
above. She had not remained long alone,
before a sound of voices in conversation met
her ear; she turned from the hedge, and, taking
her stick, limped across the little garden path
to see who were coming. Down the footpath
were proceeding leisurely two persons: Jeannette could only see their heads, on account of
the gooseberry bush which grew between, but
in this case the hat betrayed the man. She

drew back at the sight with an instinctive feeling of alarm. She had lived long enough to dread those clerical beavers, and the smooth faces that had smiled so treacherously beneath them. As she sat on her father's knee at night and drank in with thirsty ears the tales of priestly cruelty which he would detail to her with something of savage vengeance in his tone, she had learned to dread the cassock and the cowl; and so away she limped. But to her horror the priests paused at the entrance to the cottage; she heard them mention her father's name; and before she could hide herself they were upon her, and were calling to her to stop.

"Come hither, little daughter," said Brother Francis, for it was he; "come hither and tell us where your father is gone; fear not, petite."

Jeannette turned and put her finger in the corner of her mouth, and hung her head indecisively. "The voice is gentle," thought she.

The two priests approached. One stroked her head, the other admired her garland of wild flowers.

"Can you weave garlands?" he asked.

"Oh yes, I am so fond of flowers," said Jeannette.

"Ah! that is very charming," said the taller

of the two—the same priest whom Beretti dismissed so unceremoniously from the *grille* of the chapel in the château on Marie's fête-day.

Then the two priests spoke together in a language she could not follow. "Nonne melius foret hanc avertere, aut saltem temptare?" said one. "Videtur," said the tall priest, sententiously pursing up his lips. Jeannette began to fear they were going to repeat the Commandments backwards in Latin and raise the devil to carry her off. She looked about, but there was no one in sight.

"Would you like to see the flowers that hang in the great church on the hill yonder?" said Brother Francis insinuatingly.

"Oh no, monsieur, I should be afraid, for you know——" and the little one stopped suddenly and looked down on the sandalled feet of her interrogator, feeling that she had committed herself.

"You are not afraid to go, are you? Come with us and hang that garland on the sweet Mother of our Lord; won't you?"

"Who is she, monsieur? If she be *gentille*, I should be afraid."

The priests could scarcely restrain a smile at the child's simplicity.

"What! I am sure a good little girl like you knows who our Lord is—Jesus Christ, who died on the cross for little girls."

Jeannette curtseyed at the holy name, and replied warmly, "Oh! parfaitement, m'sieur; I pray to Him often, very often."

"Well done! that is right, ma chère; and do you not also pray to His sweet, kind Mother, who loves those who love her son?"

"I have never seen her—never heard father and mother talk of her."

"Ah! that is a pity. Well, if you like to come with us to the great church up there, we will show her to you, and you shall offer her those pretty flowers, and you shall ask her to help father and mother; and I doubt not the Blessed Virgin will listen to your prayers."

"I should like to ask her to bless my poor father, monsieur; he is so *triste*, now the abbé has stopped his working at the angels."

"Ah! le pauvre homme! You should pray to our Lady of Grace who lives in the great cathedral. She is very kind to little girls."

Jeannette wavered a moment between fear of the priests and the desire to benefit her parents. At last she said boldly—

"I cannot walk, you see, because I have been

ill ; but if I ·could climb up so far, I should so like to pray to the Lady——"

The tall priest ran down the steep path and beckoned one of the women to follow him. When he had brought her to Jeannette, he said—

" Madame Godet, I prythee witness what follows."

The woman thus addressed folded her arms akimbo and grinned.

Brother Francis continued his questions. " And how old are you, my little girl ? "

" I am just seven years, monsieur."

" And what is your name, ma chère ? "

"Jeannette Durand, if it please you," she said, with a curtsey.

" Take notice, Madame Godet, that Jeannette Durand is seven years old," said the tall priest, raising his forefinger.

" And why do you wish to enter yon great church ? " asked the Benedictine, with the air of a man who is about to give checkmate.

" Because, monsieur, my father is so *triste*, and I do so wish to pray to the good Mother of Jesus Christ up yonder."

The two priests turned to their witness with uplifted hands ; she in her turn ejaculated the words "Mon Dieu!" in astonishment, then ran forward and kissed Jeannette, then ran down and told her friends how little Jeannette had been converted. And when Brother Francis appeared with the little one in his arms, all the girls and women had run to the bridge to stare at her.

Madame Durand had been labouring so steadily with Marguerite that she had not noticed at first the excitement amongst the women; but when a general clatter of tongues greeted the two priests as they crossed the stream, she looked up, and, to her great amazement, saw Jeannette leaning over the Benedictine's shoulder and waving her hand. Around her pressed a crowd of women; some crying, others invoking blessings on the new disciple, and others looking half ashamed towards the poor mother whose child was being carried off " to the greater glory of God." As for Madame Durand, as she afterwards explained her feelings to a friend, she was " took all-no-how," and the marrow seemed to be trickling out of her bones; she turned white and cold, and would have fallen had not Marguerite taken her hand and helped her to a seat on the bank.

Meanwhile the priests were proceeding rapidly towards the ascent to the lime-walk, when Jeannette, who wished to kiss her mother and tell her she would not be long, cried out, " Mother ! mother ! "

The sound of her daughter's voice restored Madame Durand to sense, and, starting up with a wild scream, she ran towards the group of women who were following the priests.

" Miséricorde ! " she exclaimed. " Oh, aid me to recover my child ! "

" Hush, Madame Durand ! " said a wrinkled old hag ; " let the child be, can't you ? She wishes to be baptized, and so she shall. I advise you not to meddle with the clergy, on your life ! "

But the agonized mother took no heed of such utterances, tearing frantically through the throng to reach her child.

" Ma pauvre enfant ! " she exclaimed, seizing and covering with kisses the little wan hand that was held towards her.

" Ma mère," said the child, " do not weep ; I am only going to visit the good Lady who lives in yonder church. She will help poor father to get work."

The mother turned from her child to the

priests, who had now stopped. "Oh, sirs, by the love of God, I pray you take not my poor little sick child! Oh! if you must rob me of my children, take the elder one; she is strong and can bear it better. Do, sirs, for the love of God! do! I will call her; she is very obedient, and will be a good Catholic; but as for this little one, see! she is weak and ill."

The Benedictine could not meet the gaze of that distracted mother; he turned and faced the other women, and said, in a tone of apology—

"I call you all to witness that this child of her own consent accepted our call to quit her unhappy home, where, she tells us, the name of our Blessed Lady is never spoken; that she, being of the legal age of seven years— after which, as you know, the Holy Church is authorized to receive converts into her bosom— herself voluntarily expressed her own wish to pray to the Blessed Virgin. If, then, in consequence of the disturbance created by this turbulent and factious woman, this poor child shall change her mind, we shall pay no heed to her, believing that it is better to secure her favour with God than with man. And I call upon you all to aid us in removing our convert from the foul and pestilential atmosphere of heresy into the sweet fold of the one true Church."

This harangue was only just in time to turn the tide, which was beginning to flow with motherly instinct against the priests; and Jeannette, feeling that she had grieved her kind mother, had been sobbing and crying in the serge folds of the Benedictine's frock.

The tall priest, too, said encouragingly, and with an attempt at a smile—

"Mother Durand, don't fash yourself about the brat; she will be better cared for where she is going.   We shan't hurt her."

But Mother Durand was not to be won over by honeyed words, and stuck so tightly to the sleeve of the priest's *soutane* that he could not advance without dragging her after him.   Once more the two priests stopped, and commanded her to stand off and not impede them in the discharge of their duty.

"You may knock me down," she replied; "you may kill me if you will; but I will never let go till you give me back my child."

And the Benedictine looked as if he was ready to take her at her word; he raised his disengaged arm as if to strike, when a clear voice startled him, and made him look round.

"Fi donc, monsieur! for shame! Holà, Maintenon, à la garde!"

A moment after the mastiff sprang through a hedge which separated them from the slopes of the lime-walk, and dashed full gallop into the press, with head erect and nose in air, as if he were divining by his sense of smell which was to be his quarry. Immediately after appeared the tall, lithe figure of a young girl, whose quick breathing and flushed cheeks showed the effects of her precipitate run down the steep incline.

"Madame," shouted the monk in fury, "call off your beast of a dog, or I will cut his throat!"

Maintenon remembered his man. "I think I recollect this odour as belonging to a creature I one day found hanging about my master's study," perhaps he may have thought to himself; at any rate, he posted himself between Ethel and the monk, so as to be of service in any dental operations that might be called for. A pat from Ethel modified his aggressive attitude, and she then questioned the priests on their conduct and purpose. After hearing their account and the mother's, she tried to persuade the priests to leave the girl with her mother until the morrow. But entreaties were vain;

the more she pleaded, the more they angrily refused.

Madame Durand now threw herself at Ethel's feet and implored her not to desert her child.

" Non, madame, I will not," said Ethel, drawing herself up proudly and fronting the priests ; " they shall give you back your child."

" By St. Anthony !" shouted the monk, "if you try to hinder us, we will have you arrested as a dangerous heretic !"

" Moi ! je suis Anglaise !" said Ethel, with a defiant air.

" La peste soit des Anglaises !" muttered the tall priest to himself.

" I care not if you be Cromwell himself and all the kings of England in one !" cried the monk, beside himself with rage.

" What warrant have you for what you do ? " asked Ethel of the priests.

" The seal of the king's minister for war, madame—the great Louvois. Know ye not that the king is about to stamp out this curse from the country ? Beware, then, how you break the French laws, or your English maiden-hood may make acquaintance with a Norman prison !"

"O dear lady," cried little Jeannette, "don't let these priests carry me away from my mother. I repent me of what I said in the cabbage-garden. I did not know what I was doing. They told me the Mother of Jesus Christ lived up yonder, and she would help poor father. Oh! don't let them take me."

And the little sick child stretched out her arms in so appealing a manner that Ethel felt the blood coursing hotly in her cheeks with mingled pity and indignation. She leaned towards the child and took her hand.

The priests moved on. Jeannette had clasped Ethel's fingers tightly between both her little hands, so that she could not let go; there was a momentary struggle, in which the strain upon the child's shoulder was so great that she gave a little cry.

The mastiff, who had hitherto kept looking first at Ethel, then at the priests, scanning apparently their expressions and gestures, and yet unable clearly to understand what was the matter in dispute, no sooner perceived that it was a tussle between monk and lady as to who should possess Jeannette, than he took his side with all the promptness and enthusiasm of a young dog. Charging round to front the Benedictine, he stood upright on his hind legs and planted his forefeet on the monk's breast, snarling and showing his keen white teeth; but the monk was as brave as he was cruel, and with his disengaged hand dealt Maintenon a manly buffet on the ear. The dog shook his head, and, making a little spring forward, seized the left ear of the Benedictine in his teeth, and shook it savagely once or twice, nearly pulling the ear out of its socket. The monk screamed in agony, and let Jeannette slip down to the ground. Ethel called off the mastiff, who left his hold unwillingly, and licked the blood that clung about his lips with a savage relish.

In the confusion which followed—women rushing about in tears or offering handkerchiefs to staunch the blood—the object of all this strife was overlooked. But there was one in the crowd who thought of her. Madame Durand had snatched her up and run away with her over the green fields and across the wooden foot-bridge, and when the priests had recovered themselves enough to look for her, they only saw a retreating figure in the distance.

"You shall pay for this, mademoiselle; you

shall come before the magistrate for this. This is an illegal outrage!"

Ethel stepped aside as the monk approached, and addressing the women, who lingered about, said—

"You all bear me witness that I did not urge on the dog; and you, sir monk, beware! for if you lay a finger on me, I will say 'Holà!' to yon dog, and you will have that pretty face spoilt!" —with which withering sarcasm Ethel turned away amongst the silent admiration of the peasant-girls, who stood open-mouthed with astonishment at the audacity of "la belle Anglaise!"

But the crisis over, Ethel began to feel very uneasy as she swiftly retraced her steps to the château, and could not help looking behind her, now and then, with a sense of being pursued. Besides, she feared that her interference might bring some trouble to her friends at the château, and after long consideration she made up her mind that the whole truth must be told to the sieur before there was any possibility of its reaching his ears from any other quarter.

Maintenon had no such troublous thoughts in his head. He had dismissed the matter from his mind with the last taste of the monk's ear, and was once more the simple and light-hearted " inspector of nuisances."

CHAPTER IX.

MADAME DE CORNELLI's boudoir was constantly growing more ecclesiastical, and constantly throwing off the few remaining traces of secular life. The gay sonnets lay crumpled in a dark corner; the forgotten lute was almost reft of the potency of sound by the cruel weight of Thomas Aquinas, who sat doggedly on the strings, in two huge volumes; the riding-whip and the hawking-glove had given place to the rosary and a copy of the " Fleurs des Saints," edged with ivory.

As for the lady herself, she never stirred out but to drive to the cathedral, where she confessed and prayed, and gave alms to the poor and candles to the Virgin. And the old nurse of the family would shake her head in Constant's parlour, as she sipped the hot canary, and say—

"Dîtes donc! Monsieur Constant, take my word for it, as sure as I am a live woman, it will be a boy, a young cardinal! After all this kneeling and crying and taking on, it will be a little blear-eyed thing not fit to hold a lance or charge a musket. Aye! they may make a scholar of him, like enough, for they say his father has a marvellous good head for your Latins."

And Constant would humour the old lady with a patronising nod and a second instalment of canary, and would give her a whiff or two of tobacco to keep off the asthma.

Whilst Ethel was encountering the monk and the priest, Madame de Cornelli was encountering two devils on her *prie-Dieu* in the boudoir. These gentlemen were not visible to the naked eye, but they were none the less real in their attack upon the gentle dame, who knelt weeping, weeping, sobbing and again sobbing, with her pale face buried in her uplifted hands, and her long hair falling loosely down her back. The first devil would cross her vision, as she knelt in prayer, clad in the garb of a young nobleman. The long feather that drooped from his hat scarcely concealed the features of one with whose destiny she felt herself irrevocably linked. The black ribbon of the Order of St. Michael, the suit of embroidered taffeta fluttering with knots of many-coloured ribbons, the shoulder-belt, the long rapier, all reminded her of one for whom her heart had first known the quick pulsation of love. He was, or seemed to be, dragging her anew to the altar through a crowd of hooded nuns, who gazed upon her with a look of ineffable disdain. She struggled, but the devil's grip was too strong for her, and then there swam before her eyes a multitude of demons who taunted her with the name of "mother"—her, who might have been the spouse of Christ, unsullied by earthly love ! The vision of her husband's love swept aside, she would fall into a holy trance, and angels seemed to float over her, bearing scrolls of pardon in their hands. She would look up and smile, and reach out her white arms to take the scroll, but the angel would seem to draw back and whisper, " 'Tis for those who will forsake all and follow us." And then the second devil would rise before her, blotting out the figure of the angel which had floated in the motes of the afternoon sun, and he would hide his face with his hands and burst into an exceeding bitter cry, as one who mourned his mother. And then she would recognize the voice. "'Tis Philippe's voice," she would say to herself in a hushed tone of awe; and all her holy thoughts of surrender would be carried away in a tempest of maternal tears. Again and again these visions would recur, as, out-wearied and for-spent with prayer, she knelt in the privacy of her room.

It was some such agony of soul as this which was racking her when the door of her chamber was quietly opened and the Sieur de Cornelli stole in unobserved. His countenance was clouded with a shade of mingled doubt and sorrow, as he noticed the signs of spiritual struggle, the heaving bosom, the sob that would not be restrained. For a moment he stood irresolute; then, stepping softly to her side, he knelt and kissed her head, and placed his left arm about her, and shading his eyes with his right hand, uttered these words in a broken voice—

" O Father of Infinite Love, we come before Thee, kneeling side by side, as once we knelt before Thy altar, that Thou mightest bless our young loves and make us one. O loving Father, Thou didst bless our union in the olden time; happy years have been ours—yea, Thou hast given us the sweetest pledges to keep for Thee—the innocent babe, the priceless gem of childhood, the enthusiasm of renewed youth. Have we valued these Thy gifts as we ought? —have we watched over them to keep them pure and spotless? Lord, Thou knowest!

" Once more we kneel before Thee—we, Thy ungrateful children—asking Thee to bless us yet again! Our hearts that once were one, are sundered—sundered, good Lord, in Thy own service, in our zeal for what we hold truth. Make us one, O Lord, in Thee—one in heart and soul, and mind and affection. And if I, in my blind groping after the true Christ, have stumbled and fallen—if I am dulling the brighter mirror of her soul by the breath of my opinions—O pardon my poor unconscious errors, and grant me the help of Thy Spirit to guard me in the future, and make my soul one with her soul! And if she, O Lord, though serving Thee with much self-denial in the ministry to Thy poor, and in the strict observance of religion, shall have been led by any one to mistake her duties, and to quit the post in which Thou hast placed her for one she fancies will bring her nearer Thee, then turn her heart, O Father of Infinite Mercies—turn her heart once more to her husband and her children, and knit us together a holy family in Thee, that loving Thee we may love one another also!"

The head of the wife had fallen on the breast of the husband, and before the prayer was ended it had been heard; two sundered hearts had been re-knit, two human souls that were drifting apart for want of sympathy had explained themselves in the presence of the Searcher of all hearts.

It was some time before either spoke. The wife's heart had found a relief in tears; there, with her weary head on the bosom of him for whom she had once given up a life of courtly ease and luxury, she seemed to be whispering once more the vows she had pledged so long ago, and but now resolved to break. And it was so sweet to feel that the old love was still there, still alive and burning like a fire; so sweet to feel the old touch of the once familiar arm circling about her—that she gave herself up to the charm of the moment, like a girl that surrenders herself to some forbidden pleasure with a smile of desperate abandon. At length the sieur broke the long silence—

"We are very happy now, dearest, but it will not be for long. They will come and rear a barrier between us, those uncompromising Jesuits; they care not whose hearts be broken, so long as the Church is kept uppermost. The king has given himself up to his new mistress, and she, they say, has bargained with the Jesuits; she is to convert the old dotard to a policy of persecution, they are to consent to her marriage! Bah! I am sick of it all! Come, dearest, come away with me to a land where we can love one another without priestly interference, where your faith and mine are alike permitted. Let us flee to England, where King James will welcome you for a Catholic and his people will receive me for a Protestant. What say you, sweet? Shall I sell the château and the demesne and take you hence?"

Madame de Cornelli looked up into the face of her husband—" Mon cher, you forget, I cannot travel so far; yet, if all were well, I would even pluck up heart to carry my babe into a land of peace and safety. You tell me the English are a quiet people?"

"Quiet as sheep, ma chère! They are a nation endued with common sense, on which they pride themselves somewhat; further, they have no ideas, no grand conceptions, for which they are willing to rush to arms. They are cool

calculators; they solve the problems of existence by the rule of three, and can drink strong
ale without getting intoxicated. They value
religion, too, after a fashion: their poet turns
the Bible into blank verse, and gets rewarded
by a post under government—but that was in
Cromwell's time."

Madame de Cornelli had not listened much
to the last sentences. She was engaged in a
vision of Merrie England, where she saw herself surrounded by her family, the youngest
lying asleep in a pretty little crib adorned with
English ribbons. But the thought of her babe
suggested another idea—the mother praying
beside the cot; and the thought of prayer
called up again the thought of the Holy
Church, whose interests she had been tempted
to postpone to her own domestic happiness.

"You sigh, ma chère," said the sieur, stroking
a long yellow curl that had strayed away from
its fellows.

"Ah! if only I knew which was my duty!
God knows! I pray hourly for wisdom from
above to guide my heart aright, but the path
is beset with difficulties. Nature says, 'Follow
thy husband!'—but what if that same Nature
is a villanous fellow? Again, my confessor says,

'Save thy soul and obey the Holy Church!'—
but what if those same confessors are misled
by the spirit of party? Alas! what can a poor
weak woman do? Yet this proposal—yes, it
seems to solve the problem; quit home and
land and live abroad—but, mon cher, what will
my English confessor say to me?"

" Leave that puzzle to the day and the evil
thereof. And now hear what I propose: I
intend to despatch a courier to our good friend
La Bruyère, whose judgment in such matters
I count worth not a little; and if I can prevail
on him to pay us a visit, we can settle the
details of these transactions speedily. We
must make up our minds to sacrifice a portion
of our income, I fear; for, by all reports, the
great number of landed proprietors who have
sold all and emigrated has brought down the
price of land terribly. But half a loaf is better
than no mouth to put it in!"

With which ironical remark the sieur was
preparing to leave the chamber, when the sound
of footsteps outside arrested him. A hurried
tap at the door of the boudoir, and a hot face
thrust in, panting, startled, impatient to speak,
called forth a simultaneous cry from the sieur
and his lady.

"Mon Dieu! qu'est-ce qu'il y a, Mademoiselle
Ethel ?"

The English girl, having entered and closed
the door after her, approached her patrons
and attempted to explain to them the cause of
her perturbation ; but the speed with which she
had come up the hill, added to the agitation
consequent on the scene she had just witnessed,
caused her a momentary faintness, and she
would have slipped to the ground had not the
sieur stepped forward and supported her with
his arm.

Madame rose hastily, and, opening an antique
lacquered chest which stood in a corner of the
room, poured out a cordial in a phial and held
it to Ethel's lips. In a few moments she had
recovered herself, and, seated on a *fauteuil*,
which madame insisted she should occupy, was
narrating the events of the afternoon.

When she commenced speaking her listeners
were agitated with surprise and fear, not knowing what evil tidings the young girl was about
to produce to their own detriment. But when
the story developed itself apparently into the
troubles of a poor laundress, the look of care
had given place to an expression of com-
passionate sympathy which said, as plainly as

words could have uttered it, "Oh! it is nothing, after all. You have frightened us so, that it is quite charming to find it touches somebody else—quite charming to pity our poor neighbour!" ·

Such is human nature, even in the most unselfish. But again, as the incidents of the struggle with the clergy broke in, the sad contented look passed away on madame's face into firmly pressed lips and a colourless cheek, while the sieur rose to his feet and paced the apartment with quick, uneasy strides.

Ethel had told the story with great circumstance, dwelling largely on the poignant grief of the mother and the distress of the little sick child on finding that she was being duped, and she concluded with an indignant remonstrance against a system of conversion which proceeded by treachery and violence. So far she had proceeded without reflecting in whose presence she was speaking ; but when she concluded, and dropping her eyes saw Madame de Cornelli weeping and sobbing, she ejaculated—

"Madame, I crave your pardon. I spoke lightly. I have wounded you. I would not for worlds have spoken thus, believe me!"

" Non, mademoiselle; you have spoken the

truth, I doubt not, and the truth does wound sometimes. But think not, ma chère, that I grieve on my own account! Non! I weep for the poor stonemason and his wife, and I weep, too, for my holy religion. Monsieur, we must aid these Durands!"

"Spoken like a brave woman!" said the sieur, kissing his wife on the forehead.

"Monsieur l'Évêque will be for us, surely!" cried Ethel.

"Ah non, ma chére!" answered madame; "times are changed with monseigneur since Le Pelletier has succeeded to power. I know rfot how it is, but he always has seemed to shun me since his reverence le Père Beretti appeared on the scene."

"Yes," broke in the sieur; "the good bishop has been muzzled by the Jesuit, and, indeed, had not the Archbishop of Rouen spoken up for him, the king would have found him less comfortable quarters."

The conversation continued until the great bell rang for supper, when all took their places at the table. The rumour of Ethel's adventure had penetrated into the servants'-hall; one of the pages, in his impudent frolic, made believe his ear was bitten, as Maintenon paced with a

dignified step into the hall.   All gazed wonderingly on the fair face that had dared to confront
a monk and a priest ; Ethel felt that their eyes
were upon her, and her ears grew hot.   Marie
alone knew nothing of what had happened, and
in a low voice was rallying her companion on
her silence during supper, when the sieur said
somewhat sternly to her—

"Marie, hold your tongue! Thou wert ever
wont to babble overmuch in public.   Knowest
thou not a woman should be seen and not
heard ?"

Old Constant, who stood by with a flagon of
muscadine, unconsciously nodded his head in
approval of this sentiment.

The pages and Father Beauvais never
uttered a word all supper-time.   Marie looked
at Philippe for an explanation of the general
dismay, but his shrug of the shoulders only
added to the mystery.   Just before they rose
from the table Constant approached his master
and whispered in his ear ; he received a
whispered order and retired.

At the foot of the great staircase Ethel was
about to leave in company with Marie, when
the sieur touched her on the shoulder and
beckoned her to follow him into his study.

There she found madame already seated with
two little girls standing before her ; in the background stood a man in a blouse, and a poor
woman whom she at once recognized as
Madame Durand. They were all weeping as
the sieur entered, who closed and bolted the
door, then placed seats for Ethel and the
mason's wife, and called upon the master-mason
to say shortly what was ailing.

The gaunt, underfed *ouvrier*, thus appealed
to, wiped his eyes with the sleeve of his blouse,
and, bowing to Madame de Cornelli with a
graceful sweep of the hand, such as comes
natural to only a Frenchman, said—

"Monseigneur is doubtless aware of all that
happened when the little one there—little
Jeannette—was taken from her home. Well!
I will not repeat the story. Hélas ! the fright
of the last few hours has robbed me of my
memory ; where was I, wife ?"

Madame Durand eagerly took up the parable
and said, "Ah, le pauvre homme ! he is almost
beside himself ! Hé bien ! permit me, monseigneur, to address myself—c'est çà ! I carried
off la petite là-bas—'Jeannette,' by your ladyship's leave—into our little cottage and locked
the door ; presently up came Marguerite,

running, and saying how as all the neighbours had gone with the priests into Coutances. I unbarred the door and let her in. Then I got the large chest set up against the door as a barricade, and I up with the shutters and sat down to cry——"

"Nay, mother; you prayed to 'Our Father who art in heaven,'" broke in Jeannette, who had been carefully following the recital of events.

Madame de Cornelli smiled, and kissed the child on the forehead.

"Allons donc! well, perhaps I prayed a bit edgeways, in between the crying and the looking to the babes; but it's little poor folk can think of to say to the Almighty when there's such heavy thoughts knocking at the door of the mind, and belike I was no better than a poor Papist, muttering the Lord's Prayer over and over again——"

"Nay, mammy," urged the irrepressible lover of facts; "don't I mind your praying that father might come home safe, and didn't our Father, I mean the great 'Our Father who art in heaven,' send him to us?"

"Il est vrai!" replied the woman solemnly; "il est vrai!"

"Ah, mon Dieu!" broke in the stonemason,

with a heartrending cadence and lowered
head; "quel spectacle! No sooner had I
cried, 'It is I, open!' than the bolts were withdrawn and I saw my little girls sobbing and
hanging on to the skirts of their mother's
petticoat. But it was no time for embracing.
'Quick!' I cried; 'put on your cloaks, our lives
are in danger! They pursued me with yell and
blow through the town, shouting out that we
were an accursed family, and they would fire
our kennel over our heads.'"

"Oui, madame," interrupted the mason's
wife, "it was so indeed; and le pauvre homme!
he was bleeding and out of breath as he spoke.
I just wiped his face and got my little ones
ready, put our few *deniers* together in a scrip,
and away we started, like so many hunted
rabbits."

As the several portions of this narrative were
being pieced in by the members of the Durand
family, Madame de Cornelli was growing more
and more sympathetic. Little Jeannette, who
was leaning against her chair, was at last fain to
look up in childish surprise, when from stroking
the little head madame suddenly passed to
pulling the child to her bosom and covering her
with kisses.

The effect upon the sieur was different. As
the story was concluded he stood erect, his eyes
fixed into space, his lips compressed. You
might have taken him for a statue; but the
curving nostrils and heaving breast told of a
living passion, controlled but not tamed. And
if you had gazed into those eyes you would
have met—not the vacant, far-off look of the
student, but the flashing indignant glance of
one who resolves to strike the blow his conscience imperiously demands.

There was a silence of some minutes, broken
at length by the mason saying, "And so we
turned our steps here, not knowing where we
could better go for succour than to the wise
and kind lord of the Château de l'Esprit."

"Oui, madame," chimed in the childish voice
of Jeannette; "I said the great lady would
protect me, though she is a Papist, because she
is good to the poor, and—and you know the
great Lady up yonder in the cathedral, don't
you?"

"Who, my child? What lady mean you?"

"The Lady they told me about—the good
Mother of our Lord."

Madame de Cornelli laughed and cried by
turns. "She is but half a Huguenot, monsieur!" she cried to the sieur.

"So much the better, ma chère; our sympathies are united."

Then the conversation turned on the various plans of escape or concealment which offered themselves. After several had been discussed, Durand suddenly cried out—

"I think I know of something that may help us, if monseigneur will permit me to follow him to the white tower which my grandfather built for one of monseigneur's ancestors."

"The white tower!" exclaimed the sieur. "That is no longer fit for men's habitation; its rooms are lumbered up with fire-wood, and the bats and owls have made their homes therein."

"It is well!" rejoined the mason; "but if monseigneur would conduct me thither, I could tell him more anon."

Accordingly De Cornelli rang a hand-bell, which was answered by one of the pages, who was commanded to bid Constant wait with the keys of the château. "You, madame, wait our return, with this poor woman and her children, and bid the attendants serve her with a repast."

So saying, the sieur led the way to the great staircase, where Constant was already awaiting his approach with two hands laden with old and rusty keys, which he was jangling disconsolately, and all the more so because in his room had been gathered all the gossips of the servants' quarters to discuss, mystify, and exaggerate the details of news which had filtered into the château through the mouths of such dignitaries as the barber and apothecary, whose custom it was to call at the château three or four times in the week. To be called away, therefore, at such an inauspicious time, when a flagon of good cider had only just been broached, was enough to cloud the brow of one less sensual than the *maître d'hôtel*. But his bow was none the less reverential as his master approached, though in raising his head he took occasion to glance sharply at the figure in the blouse and wooden *sabots*, as much as to say, "Par la mort, non, le diable!" And when Durand paused on the first step of the well-polished staircase and seemed to consider whether it would not be better to remove his *sabots*, old Constant murmured "C'est juste!" and nodded to him to take off the obnoxious articles.

On reaching the second floor they passed along a corridor which communicated with the sleeping chambers of the women servants, through which latter they had to pass before reaching a heavily barred oak door, which had evidently not been opened for some time, for the spiders had spun their net-work of chains about and across it. Here Constant took out a large iron key, and turning it with difficulty, let the sieur and the mason through into a circular stone chamber, which was in fact a staircase in the said white tower.

"Remain here, Constant, and give me the keys," said the sieur.

The *maître d'hôtel* handed over a small bunch of keys, and signed to Durand to replace his *sabots*.

The noisy clack of the *sabots* as they passed up the staircase died away on the wondering ears of the good Constant. "Hé, mon petit Dieu! there is a frolic toward now! Yes; they have stopped at the top flooring but one—the old sieur's tool-house and workshop. Ha! I have lost the sounds!"

But the sieur and Durand were discussing the propriety of making Constant privy to their secret. The result was that the old *serviteur* was invited to join them, for it was clearly imprudent to leave him conscious of a mystery

which his curiosity might prompt him to unravel
of his own account ; neither had his master any
reason to doubt his fidelity.

When, then, Constant entered the chamber,
which, as he had rightly guessed, the two others
were examining, he found Durand standing on
the iron dogs which lay embedded in the cold
hearth-stone, his head some way up the wide
chimney, and a sepulchral voice saying, " I
think I've found it."

" It is a secret-door he is looking for, which
is to lead us to a chamber where he and his
family may rest secure a while."

" Oui, oui, monseigneur," replied the old
servant, stooping to catch a glimpse of the
mason's upper regions.

" I never knew of it, Constant, till he told
me this evening. Have you ever heard of it
in my father's time ? "

" Mais non ! to be sure your honoured father
was much up here with his hand-saws and axes,
but as no one ever saw much result of his noble
labours, it was reported that the poor gentleman
was a little wrong in his wits, begging your
pardon ; but if he came here to have private
interviews with secret guests, of course that
explains the old gentleman's oddities. Many a

time have I swept a day's shavings into my pocket."

"Strange!" said the sieur, tapping with his knuckles the panels of the wall.

Almost at the same moment Durand reappeared, somewhat glorified with a halo of mortar about his head.

"I have found the entrance, an iron shutter about four feet above this stone, which is fastened down with screws. With a driver I can lay it open in six minutes."

It was agreed that Constant should fetch the required tools, and at the same time summon Pierre and Philippe, that if any extra assistance was required they might lend it.

There was a staircase leading to the base of the tower, from which in former times an exit had been made by a small postern ; but this door had long been disused, and secured from the inside by two heavy beams being nailed across it. The room on the ground floor had been made a deposit for fire-wood and old casks, and to re-open the communication, it was necessary first to make a passage through the logs and butts, and then to knock off the planks of fir which barred the door.

When Constant returned with his two allies

this work was promptly put before them, while
Durand and the sieur remained above to pene-
trate the mysteries of the secret chamber.   By
means of a short ladder it was easy to gain a
firm footing on a level with the iron shutter
which closed the passage ; but when the screws
were withdrawn it required almost more than
one man's strength to hold it up.   A torch had
been procured, and Durand, forcing his body
through the half-open aperture, uttered a cry of
surprise and drew back.

" Ma foi ! what is it ? " said the sieur sharply.

Durand whispered, " There is some one
there ! "

" Nonsense, the place has no other entrance
but this."

" Oui, vraiment ! there is a little window at
the further end, half covered with ivy, and by
it sits a lady ! "

The chimney in which the sieur was groping
was dark.   Durand's words made his flesh
creep; yet he cried again, " Nonsense ! " but this
time in a hushed tone, as if he spoke against
his will.

Durand held up the shutter and the sieur
peered into the chanber.

Yes ; there sat a lady, leaning forward on

a little table! The sieur gathered up courage to cry, " Hein! Madame!" An owl looked out of the ivy and blinked his eyes, but the lady said never a word.

CHAPTER X.

THE presence of the mysterious lady in the secret chamber of the white tower so terrified the mason that neither taunts nor entreaties could induce him to make an entrance. Even the sieur himself, with all his erudition and sagacity, was not proof against a feeling of awe, as he thought to himself that the chamber might well be tenanted by right of prescription by some such devil as mocked Martin Luther, or another such spirit as tempted Saint Anthony.

It was agreed that 'twere better to call up the others, as it was well known that old Pierre had encountered more than one hobgoblin triumphantly—according to his own showing. Durand therefore descended to the basement and told the marvellous story, and in a few seconds Philippe was standing by his father's side, panting with the exertion of his run upstairs, his hungry eyes wide open and sparkling with boyish glee as he climbed to peer into the strange chamber. But he came down the ladder with a pale face, and said no word to Pierre, who asked him had he seen aught; only he motioned to him to put foot to the rounds of the ladder.

" I had a dream last night. Methought an archangel or two stood by my truckle-bed and said, ' Pierre, fear not ! go on in the strength of the Word, and the Scarlet Woman shall not prevail ! ' Yes, my masters; by the help of the Word will we do great things."

So saying Pierre ascended the ladder, carrying in his left hand an open Bible, as a talisman against the machinations of the foul fiend. Durand forced the iron shutter half open, and the coachman thrust his head and shoulders into the gloomy room. Those below could faintly catch the sound of his voice, as he plied the unknown intruder with texts from all the minor prophets, interlarding his remarks with a few objurgatory epithets collected from the history of Jezebel. But at last he returned, shaking his head, and vowing it was no every-day fiend that could resist such spiriting.

" Go in thyself, Pierre, and take her by the

throat," said the sieur, with a sly smile at his son, for he began to doubt the far-famed courage of Jehu. "Go in, and put the fiend to shame!"

"Nay, my master, that would be to tempt God and put in jeopardy the Christian's armour; the breast-plate of election and the sword of personal godliness may not be lightly exposed to trial." Then, a gleam of common-sense shooting, as it so often did, across the old Calvinist's weather-stained features, he added, "Let us put the dog at her; I'll warrant him to test her whereabouts!"

The proposal was received with general applause, the very idea of a dog being sufficient to break the spell that was tightening their chests, and quickening their foolish pulses, and robbing their muscles of power and their nerves of directing energy. "Aye, aye, the dog! then we shall know all about her!"

"Mon père," said Philippe, as they stood awaiting the arrival of Maintenon, "you have often told me not to fear the presence of evil spirits, but what think you now?"

"Wait a little and see the end. I have my suspicions as to the nature of this strange phantom-trove, which, if not flesh and blood, will at least prove to be bone, methinks; but here they come with the dog."

Maintenon stepped into the room with just the subdued swagger of a town physician when he is ushered into a consulting-room full of rural practitioners. It was somewhat troublesome to get him up the steps to see his patient, and he made pretence of biting the friendly hand which pushed him from behind; but when he was shown the narrow slit through which it was expected he would make his entrance, the spirit of adventure stirred his canine blood, and he leaped into the haunted room with tail erect and nose in air.

"He doesn't see her, le coquin!" cried Constant.

"Peste!" said the mason; "then it is a fiend!"

But suddenly the dog, who had been vaguely casting about, caught sight of the figure and gave a low growl, stopped, barked, advanced growling within two feet of the dress, stopped growling and sniffed the air, then came back with his tail down to the iron shutter, half growling, half whining, but always facing the figure of the woman.

In a moment the sieur had jumped down

into the room, patted the dog, and walked up to the front of the seeming fiend. Constant was uttering his *credo*; Pierre held his Bible towards his master; the mason was holding back Philippe, who wished to share his father's danger. In a few minutes the sieur came back.

"The mystery is solved; it is as I thought!"

"Oh! tell me, papa; what is it?" cried Philippe.

"A skeleton of a woman! been there fifty years, I should say."

By this time the others had so far recovered their nerve as to jump down into the room, and all were busy prowling round the skeleton with exclamations of surprise; but Maintenon alone kept his tail down in the presence of Death, and refused to stir.

Tenderly they lifted her up, this phantom of the buried past, and bore her with care to an upper chamber in the tower until a grave could be prepared for her and the dirge should be chanted over her remains; but with all the gentle handling enjoined by the sieur, it could not be helped if fragments of the decayed robes fell like gossamer to the ground.

While the "haunted chamber," as it was now

called, was being prepared for the reception of the Durand family, the sieur had rejoined his wife, called her to her boudoir, and told her the strange incident which had just befallen. There was no clue to the mystery, no tradition in the family that threw light on the discovery of this unburied skeleton, and upon Madame de Cornelli the event bore with no little weight of apprehension, steeped as she was to the lips in the spirit of the times, which heard a goblin in the creaking of every door, and saw a mysterious messenger from heaven or hell in every mote that danced before the eyes of the dyspeptic. But De Cornelli himself had in great measure emancipated himself from the thrall of such superstitions, having studied early and late amongst such authors as Des Cartes, Malebranche, Torricelli, Huygens, and the English philosopher, Bacon. Yet the most sceptical of your scientific men will feel uneasy at the discovery of a skeleton in his house, and that, too, not smuggled away in the proverbial cupboard, but resting fleshless elbows on a table in one of his private apartments!

However, the necessity for action in respect to the family of the master-mason left him no time to puzzle out the explanation of this

untoward circumstance, and when, shortly,
Constant appeared at the door announcing that
all was ready, he jumped up from his seat,
where he had been musing, and, dashing his
hand across his eyes, gave orders for the household to be summoned in the entrance hall so
soon as Pierre should bring round the covered
wagon, as he had been before instructed to do.
This done, he himself saw to the preparation of
the little girls, as for a long journey, providing
packets of cheese and fruit and apples, and
clothing them with warm cloaks.

There was the usual bustle in the hall when
the covered wagon drew up at the stone steps
as there was at the departure of the high
nobility. The pages ranged themselves on
either side of the door, the footmen hurried
to and fro with lanthorns and wrappers, and
the *femmes-de-chambre* peeped out coyly from
behind the stone pillars. Nor was there less
curiosity to see the little peasant girls whom
their master delighted to honour, the heroes of
the hour, the victims of priestly tyranny. And
many a *bon voyage* was whispered them as
they pattered across the floor in their little
wooden *sabots*.

"Reserve your horses up the hills, Pierre; 'tis

a long way from here to the village of Gran-
ville," said the sieur, in a voice loud enough to
be heard by his servants.

"Trust Pierre to take care of his own cattle!"

"Adieu!" And the lights flashed and the
wheels grated on the gravel, and the great door
was closed with a bang, and the little hunted
children with their parents were off—whither?

At a corner of the drive, not many paces
from the château, Philippe was awaiting the
chariot. Down stumbled the master-mason,
sardonically smiling; from her comfortable
corner stole forth the mason's wife, bewildered
but submissive, and the little ones rubbed their
eyes saying, "Are we there so soon?" But
Philippe hushed them all to silence, and led
them swiftly through the old postern in the
white tower, up the steps and to the foot of the
ladder which rested on a hearth-stone and
seemed to lead to the stars. Here a little
coaxing was needed to fortify them to the
ascent; but when they saw the red coals glowing
in the brazier, and the curtained beds prepared
for them in the haunted room, they were
content, and the iron shutter was closed upon
the concealed Huguenots.

As for Pierre, he lashed his leaders fiercely

through the drive, and then, by a by-road, drove quietly home, and incontinently stabled his wondering horses!

The lights were twinkling in the upper windows of the château, though it was long after the time when its inmates were usually snug in bed; for many words and much shrugging of knowing shoulders had followed the departure of the fugitives. The sky was overcast with thick clouds, and from over the sea came every now and then a flash of lurid light which lit up terrace and grey battlement and rustling beech with a momentary splendour. Under one of the great trees, which threw its black arms across the drive, stood two figures contemplating the upper portion of the white tower; they spoke in a low tone, and seemed to be listening for the sound of approaching steps.

"Mais, mon père," said the shorter of the two, "will it not be possible for the Papists to discover them by the light which will issue from the window?"

"Not at all," answered the sieur. "Durand has lights in his chamber even now, and yet we get no ray from yonder tower. I took care to examine into that before I left the chamber, and I found that the aperture which serves for window is built somewhat like a funnel, curving so that from within you cannot see what passes outside, and from without you cannot mark the light which burns in the chamber. And the boughs of yonder beech, together with the ivy which climbs about the wall, effectually screen the place from observation—but hark!"

As he spoke, the tramp of feet was heard in the distance, and the yelping of Pierre's poodle at the entrance gates, and the lowing of some cattle that had been disturbed in their first sleep, betokened an intrusion.

"Ah! they come!" whispered the boy fiercely, and grasped his stout ash-stick tightly. But his father seized him by the arm and hurried him by a side-door into the servants' quarters.

They passed quickly to the room where Constant was wont to receive his company, and where they found him now mopping his forehead with a dirty dish-cloth, while a page was reading by the light of an oil lamp in a soiled volume of Rabelais.

The entrance of the sieur was so noiseless that neither the *maître-d'hôtel* nor the page noticed it, and the dark, handsome features of the latter were breaking out into a private grin of secret amusement, when the sieur clapped him sharply on the shoulder. " Allons donc! they are coming!"

The boy dropped the book on the lamp in his alarm; the lamp went out, and the group were left in darkness.

" Sapristi!" ejaculated Constant, who had not recognized the voice of his master; " in the name of the Almighty, avaunt!"

The sieur took up the flint which he wore suspended round his neck by a gold chain, and deftly lighted the tinder which hung beside it. " Here! Constant, relume the extinguished lamp, while I give Adolphe his orders—and you, silly boy, gather your wits together that have gone a rollicking with yon madcap satirist."

The boy blushed, ashamed of having started like a coward, but proud of having been singled out on some secret service on this night of all others.

" Tenez, Adolphe; you are to go out and lurk under the shadow of the cedars, a bow-shot from the château, and when you hear steps advancing, go meet the intruders and offer to betray my secret. Tell them how Pierre drove off with the fugitives in the direction of Avranches, and use thy discretion to get them away as soon as possible. Vite! allez! they are even now crossing the park."

The boy seized his hat and bounded off with alacrity; the others went to the scullery window which faced that way, and unbarring a shutter, listened and peeped through the gloom of the whispering night.

There was not a moment to lose. A procession of men and boys was even now in sight of the château: the first rank carried two lanthorns hung on high poles, which served more to make them visible than to render them able to see. In the centre walked two persons in the uniform of his Majesty, with cocked hat, and sword dangling at the belt. Two or three priests' frocks were there, some *ouvriers* in the pay of the clergy, and a rabble of boys eager to pocket any valuable that Saint Fortuna would throw in their way. Adolphe could just make out so much by the dim light of the swaying lanthorns, as he emerged from the shadow of the trees.

" Halte! and look well to your arms there behind!" said a voice, which Adolphe recognized as that of André, the tax-collector.

" Messieurs, it is a friend," cried Adolphe, " that is, if you are good Catholics."

"Welcome friend," replied one of the cocked hats. "What is your business?"

"First tell me what is yours here," said Adolphe.

Thereupon arose a consultation between the two cocked hats, and a reference to a monk who carried a stout cord. At last André said—

"If it be that you are a friend of this company, pray how know you that you so be?"

"I have been hoping and expecting that the town of Coutances would send to fetch those children of the devil."

A deep "Ah!" burst from the invading army, who had now, out of curiosity, surrounded the page, and each one who had ejaculated the loudest turned at once to chide and silence his neighbour.

"Then they are here?" asked André.

"Pas du tout, messieurs, that is what I wish to come to; but, pardon me, speak low or my lord will overhear us, and then I am ruined. No! they were conveyed to Avranches this very night by that old heretic Pierre. See! the road is marked by the trampling of the hoofs, for they tore away as if hell were let loose at their tails."

The lanthorns were lowered, the inspection of the track bore out the page's story. There was a silence of some seconds, then some one cried—

"Break open the doors of the heretic, the cursed Huguenot!"

Adolphe put his finger to his lips. "There is a curse hanging to the old house; a dead body has been found this evening in the white tower yonder—the skeleton of a woman. We used to hear her sing at midnight, and knew not whence the sounds came; now she has been discovered, and she lies yonder. Hårk! is not that her note?"

Teeth were chattering in the heads of the invaders by this time.

The night had been growing darker, as the thunder-cloud rode grimly in the western sky, and distant mutterings of thunder came to the ears of the persons who stood beneath the sieur's cedar-trees.

"'Twere best to hurry home before we get a drenching," quoth one greybeard.

"Dame! why sleep we not to-night in my lady's alcoves?" asked a petulant youngster.

"Nay," replied André, "I will never make one to break the king's peace. Mark me, mes braves garçons, her ladyship has good interest at court, and it behoves us to be moderate in our actions and wary in our policy."

There was a suppressed titter among the boys, with whom the moderation of the tax-collector passed under the name of cowardice. But as they turned to retrace their steps a monk took Adolphe aside.

"Tell me, young man, have they sent the English demoiselle away, too?"

Adolphe paused ere he replied, not that a lie came unwillingly to his lips, but he scarcely knew how to answer.

The monk shook him by the arm, and repeated his question.

"Peste!" replied the boy savagely; "since you will have it, know that mademoiselle it is who lies dead in the white tower!"

"Dead! c'est impossible! I never saw one so full of life and health."

"Mais, c'est vrai! We bury her, la pauvre fille, to-morrow."

There were lights burning long past midnight in the lodgings of the Jesuit confessor. The bishop's old mother, who could not sleep for fear of the lightning, saw across the gardens of the bishop's residence a head looking out again and again from the father's window, and she said to herself, " He too, le pauvre homme, fears the storm."

Good, innocent old mother!—with your simple readings of human nature and distrust in that special Providence to whose protection you commend your life with faith (when the stars are out and heaven flies no danger-signal) —it is not thunder and lightning that Beretti fears to-night. The storm he watches is one of his own brewing, and whether his lightning will strike down the object of his aim or no, that is the doubt which keeps him pacing so uneasily about his chamber. Before him on the table lies a pile of papers; he cannot forbear stopping now and then to read them to himself, and to make audible comments on their contents.

" Order from the chief magistrate for the arrest of Durand, wife, and two children. Item for arrest of Ethel Digby—good! Charges against the Sieur de Cornelli . . . item against his serviteur Pierre. Aye! these last will, like good wine, improve with keeping."

The smile of satisfaction that played about his thin lips, like March sunshine on a gusty day, soon passed away, and he stood gazing with dark, melancholy eyes into the night; the heavy drops were pattering on the gravel-walk beneath his window, and the thunder was snarling and growling in the distance.

"It was such a night as this my mother died! Hey! what struggles of heart and mind has thy poor son gone through since then! I was to walk with Jesus—those were her words —I was to go about doing good!"

A haggard face turned from the window, a deep sigh broke the stillness of the room, then the young Jesuit knelt by his hard bed and sobbed. When he rose from his knees there was a look of firm resolve in his eye.

"God pardon me!" he muttered to himself; "my heart is almost too womanish to do Thy will, O God! I confess I have grown to love that family; and to disturb the peace of that sweet mother, at such a critical period, too, for her, gives my foolish heart a pang. Yet both for her and him it must be best as it is ordained—better far that she should be weaned from her love of him before her soul is imperilled; better for him to suffer confiscation, the loss of home and wife and children, if haply his erring soul may be led by such chastisement to the bosom of the Church; better, at all events, to be punished in this world than in the world to come. Aye! it would be a fond weakness to spare the rotten branch and so spoil the foliage of a goodly tree. Heart! heart! steel thyself to do justice, as thou lovest mercy! See how the divine lightning yonder cleaves the gallant oak in its ruthless career—cleaves the oak and the minaret on consecrated roof, the holy friar and lewd gallant, with impartial stroke; storm and tempest fulfilling His word, clearing away the ill vapours from the sky, healing the general disease, and unmindful of what particular injury may befall by the way. Aye! that is it! So must the true servant of the Church work, looking only to the end, with humble faith and perseverance untired."

The young Jesuit again went to the window and looked forth. The clouds had broken, and the moon was riding peacefully in a field of blue sky; the inky clouds were packed close to right and left, yet the rain no longer fell in torrents, but softly as the gentle dew from heaven. Beretti came back to the table and looked at his chronometer, and muttered—

"Three of the clock! Then they must be spending the night at the château! Yet I charged Brother Francis to return."

" Pax vobiscum! here am I—if indeed this dripping rag be myself."

Beretti looked up and saw standing in the doorway the figure of the monk; his cowl, drawn over his head, was soaked with rain, which, indeed, was streaming from him at all points, and the steam from his damp and heated body visibly rose to the ceiling.

After a few words of surprise and explanation, the monk recited to his superior the issue of the adventure, enlarging upon the cowardice of the tax-collector and the certainty that the Durand family had been removed; but when the Benedictine mentioned the sudden death of the young English girl, Beretti put down the pen with which he had been taking notes of the monk's narration, and cried—

" Hold, brother, that smacks of falsehood; I cannot accept it!"

" The page who told me seemed deeply moved, else had I too thought it all incredible; and he added that she was to be interred to-morrow."

" Then shall I assist at her obsequies!" said the Jesuit; " good-night!"

CHAPTER XI.

THE morning broke sweet and fresh, with a soft wind from the sea which wafted the scent of autumn flowers from many a ripening field, and ruddy-faced apples and tapering pears glistened among the dripping leaves in the early morning twilight. But it was neither autumn fragrance nor orchard fruits that had drawn old Pierre so early from his bed this Sunday morning; he stands a little behind the right wing of the château with one of the gardeners, right amongst the apple-trees and in the long rich grass, favoured by the shade to reach a luxuriancy unknown to other soils. The old coachman puts his head now on this side, now on that, as if he were debating some question of great nicety, while the gardener, with shouldered spade, awaits the oracular response. " Bien ! she will do very nicely here—

and hurry yourself, for she is to be in the temple at half-past six."

"Aye, aye, Master Pierre; I'll get two men to help dig her out as pretty a snuggery as ever you see. Dear, dear! to think so comely a young lady should come to so untimely an end!"

"All flesh is grass," replied Pierre, as he measured out, foot by foot, the needful length for a grave, "and your turn may be the next."

"That's very true, Master Pierre; but is the master going to have a burial service over her, or how?"

"Monsieur le Pasteur has been sent for, since he, thou knowest, has no temple now at Coutances to demand his services; and to-day the elect will worship in our private temple here—after that, elsewhere, for the servants of God are grievously tormented. And that reminds me, last night's drive in the wet has brought on my old rheumatism; but I have much to be thankful for, I have much to be thankful for."

The two *serviteurs* departed in search of men to dig the grave.

Let us now enter the château. The servants are astir, but not with their wonted gaiety of

manner, for the natural carelessness of tem-
perament which is characteristic of the Gallic
race has evidently been sobered into a thoughtful fear by some moral shock. They open the
shutters noiselessly, and glide about the wooden
floors as if they were afraid to wake the dead
echoes of a horrible past ; they swallow their
words again before they have well left the
throat, with a painful spasm of remembered
awfulness. It is the old, old blossoming of the
selfish panic, " I may be taken next!"

When the page returned to his master and
told him the trick he had played upon the monk
in making him believe that Miss Digby was dead,
it occurred to the sieur that at all events it might
be prudent to let this belief get about for a few
days, till either the affair blew over or he could
send her to some place of safety. Constant
and Pierre were therefore informed of the plan,
as they of course had been present at the discovery of the skeleton in the white tower.

In the middle of the night Marie was aroused
by some one tapping her shoulder ; starting up
she met her father's gaze. He bade her get up
and acquaint Ethel with the state of affairs, telling his daughter in a few words what had
occurred, and urging the necessity of Ethel's

leaving her bedroom before the house was astir in the morning.

Ethel slept in an ante-room opening into Marie's, and hearing voices she had risen, wrapt herself in a travelling-cloak, and peeped into the bed-chamber. She was about to retire on seeing the sieur, but he beckoned her to stay, and, apologizing for the intrusion at such an hour, put the whole case before her, and requested her to make a hasty retreat to another part of the house. In a few minutes she was ready, and, passing the doors of the *serviteurs*, who slept still a heavy morning sleep, the two entered the white tower as noiselessly as they could.

The sieur did not take her to the secret chamber, thinking that it was unlikely the château would be searched, now the clergy had been put off the scent, but he left her in the room which communicated with it. After revealing to her the secret passage by the chimney, and placing some cushions for her to recline on, he bade her good-night, and assured her that though she was now no more, yet her breakfast should not be forgotten.

At half-past six in the morning the bearers had carried an open bier into the temple, as

the sieur's private chapel was called. Marie
and Philippe were there, and the sieur and
many of his servants, men and women. The
aged Pasteur la Rose mounted into a pulpit by
a circular staircase concealed in a tower of
wood, painted to imitate marble, and from the
loge, as it seemed, of this tower of vantage
addressed a few simple words to his hearers on
the subject of sudden death. This done, the
bier, covered with flowers and sprigs of holly
and bay, was once more carried, as the custom
was, low down and at arm's length between the
bearers, to the gray morning light and the long
waving grass beneath the orchard trees.

Then, as soon as the bier had been lowered
into the shallow grave, and the gardeners had
shovelled some handfuls of earth on the top, and
the servants had pressed round and dropped,
some a tear, and some a flower, and some a
word or two of whispered farewell, La Rose
held up his hand and prayed, but in silence, for
the law forbade him to pray aloud at funerals,
and the rest stood still with bended heads and
moving lips, in silent prayer.

As they stood thus, one approached the
grave, coming from under the apple-trees,
checking his hasty stride as he saw how the

little band of mourners was engaged, but yet
stealing to the crumbling verge, and peeping
over at the mingled earth and flowers which
lay below.　He was clothed in domino and
long cassock, and a thick girdle of twisted silk
was tied round his middle and fell almost to the
ground.　He crossed himself and murmured a
prayer like the rest.

La Rose, who had stood all the time with up-
raised hand, had no sooner let it fall than all
heads were raised and eyes uplifted to the
stranger's face.　La Rose himself looked inquiringly at the sieur, and then furtively at the
stranger, as if he were uncertain what part he
ought to take ; but De Cornelli, bowing courte-
ously, spoke in a subdued voice—

" His reverence the Father Beretti does us
the honour of praying at our funeral."

Beretti held out his hand and replied, in
a louder tone—

" Over an open grave we can have but few
differences, and I, at least, may pray for the
dead."

For a few moments the mourners lingered,
looking down with bewildered eyes upon what
seemed to them the ruins of a young life prematurely arrested.　But when all were gone

except the pasteur, De Cornelli roused the Jesuit from his musings thus :—

"Father Beretti, with you I cannot stoop to any act of deception. You think you are looking on the grave of a young girl ; so the *serviteurs* believe, so the story has got about through the mischievous drollery of one of my pages, who wished to throw dust in the eyes of your priests. For myself, I have not spoken to any one as yet, either in favour of or against this theory; and if I have not refuted it, it is because I am desirous to allow mademoiselle time to effect her escape from the pursuit of the—the authorities. The fact is, the occupant of this grave is as unknown to me as to you. Yesterday, in making some researches in a neglected part of the château, we came across a few unburied bones, which this morning you find us rendering to mother earth. Now, I am frank with you when I might have deceived you, and I look to find you generous towards this English lady, who has been betrayed by a natural impulse into an act of imprudence."

"Imprudence ! an act that might well send her to the Bastille, monseigneur ; but I pass that by. So far as I am concerned she is safe ; for, as you say, she is young and has not been born or bred amongst us, so that it could do no good to visit penalties upon her. So much for the astuteness of the Benedictine!" And the Jesuit laughed to himself at the thought of Brother Francis's discomfiture, when he heard how he had been outwitted.

The sieur and the Jesuit did not long remain in company; theirs was a courtesy so thin-skinned that the volcano of religious differ-ence might at any moment burst the crust, and pour forth the lava of angry discussion. The priest sought the apartments of Father Beauvais, the sieur went to his studio.

After the morning service in the Catholic chapel, and whilst the Huguenots, who held their service at a later hour, were engaged in fervid psalm-singing, it happened that Father Beretti and Madame de Cornelli and her daughter were met together in the red boudoir. Madame was reclining on the sofa, as had been her wont of late, and Marie was lightly touching the harpsichord as she murmured to herself the words of a song once admired by one now absent. Beretti was pacing with measured tread up and down the apartment, conning aloud a breviary which he held in his right hand. So fast did he mouth it, that an heretical observer would surely have deemed he was racing through the office for a wager. But not so thought madame, whose eyes stole with a soft beam of content from the absorbed priest to the pensive daughter, filled with the warm flood of thankfulness to God for the blessings of a religious home and beautiful children, and, when they had filled their cups to the brim, let fall one unnoticed tear for her erring lord.

When the Jesuit had completed his task, closed the well-thumbed book, and replaced it in his breast, Madame de Cornelli said—

"I have been thinking, my father, whether it may not be mistaken policy on the part of our Church to try and coerce these so-called Reformed. My husband, I know well, has many points of agreement with us; his large and sympathetic heart beats true to much that we cherish, and in joining the Huguenots I do believe that he is mainly led by a passionate love of freedom. Give him liberty to think as he will, and you will find him in most points your ally; but once put a string about your falcon's leg, and he will, in his struggle to free himself, get sundered from you for ever. I may be wrong, father—indeed, of course I must, since the Holy Church is guided by God's Vicar on earth, who may not err; but I want to hear you explain to me how it is that the Church thus makes use of an iron compulsion."

Marie had ceased to warble her wayward notes as her mother spoke, and sat with parted lips and that piquant arching of the eyebrows that became her so well, waiting for the Jesuit to explain a difficulty which had occurred to her too.

The father drew a chair near the sofa, gazed with a long, wistful gaze, full of a half-sad tenderness, into the eyes ·of the lady, ere he replied—

"Dear sisters in the faith, a little opening of the eyes is a dangerous thing! One of two things must we do, would we avoid the precipice of religious error: either shut our eyes, as the Italian women do when they cross the mountain-pass on their mules, trusting to our religious guides to guide our steps in the way of truth; or, if we can, study man and nature, mind and matter, schoolmen and theologians, philosophers of the *à priori* or of the *à posteriori* method—your Des Cartes and your Roger Bacons, your great historians, your little ballad-makers, your clever Montaignes, your Charrons, your Fénélons, your Torricellis; in fact, whatever serves to throw light on truth and error.

When you have done this, and opened the eyes
of your understanding, such questions as these
which you raise for my debating will assume
their due proportion ; they will no longer be the
idle questioning of a mind half disposed to
scepticism."

Madame de Cornelli's eyes were beginning
to fill with tears. The Jesuit proceeded in a
softer tone, resting his hand on hers—

"Nay, my daughter ; I know your heart is
right before God, and I only sound its depths
by casting in my harmless pebble. No common
temptations are surrounding you, and it will task
all our prayers to preserve you from falling
away ; and, sweet friend, those prayers shall not
be wanting. I would not fatigue you with long-
drawn arguments to show you how those who
hold the truth are bound to maintain it, at the
cost even of precious human lives. If we do
not allow our citizens to spread abroad fevers
and plagues and such things as hurt the body,
how much less should we tolerate them who go
about to poison men's souls, and beget for them
the pains of purgatory ? But to quit the theory
and come to facts. Know ye, my sisters, that
the liberty that these pestilential heretics desire
is but the license to destroy our freedom. They

reck nought of liberty of thought, save as touching their own opinions, and when the freedom they ask is granted, straight run they to put down with violence the religious liberty of all who differ from them. Shall I recall to your recollection the hundred and twenty Catholics killed at Nismes by these offscourings, in the year of grace 1567? Or, if that seemeth too far away, shall I tell you how one Ferrier, in the same glorious, antique city, was, in 1613, excommunicated by his own heretical body for simply speaking ill of Protestant synods? Nay, the words of the act which commanded his expulsion are worthy of the attention of such as think the dogmas of Geneva inculcate liberty of conscience. It ran thus, if I remember aright: 'We, in the name and power of our Lord Jesus Christ, by the conduct of the Holy Ghost, and with authority from the Church, have cast him off from the society of the faithful, that he may be delivered up to Satan.' There! is not the style truculent enough to suit the secret counsels of the Vehmic tribunals of Westphalia? Oui, mes amies; and to show the poor fellow they were in earnest, these Huguenots sacked his house at night, and sent him naked out of the city! Then, again, look at Condé's rebellion in the year 1615, when these tolerated Huguenots tried to crush our holy religion, and overpower his most sacred majesty the king; but by the grace of God it was soon put down. And Rochelle, the stronghold of the Reformed religion (so-called), affords the most amazing proof of their intolerance. In 1620 the great assembly, of which Rohan and Mornais, you know, were the leading spirits, passed a law confiscating the goods of all Catholics; and there, where the mistaken clemency of the king had allowed the Protestants freedom of worship, the same measure of freedom was refused to Catholics, and no Catholic church was allowed within the walls of the city. But to leave great measures and come to the amenities of life, which ladies know so well how to estimate, what think you of a freedom which forbade theatres and dancing, which proscribed all gay colours in dress, and all plaiting of the hair? Why, the very pasteurs themselves must confine their learning to Hebrew, avoiding the sound of Greek, as being, forsooth, a profane tongue! No smattering of science might they obtain through chemistry, or such like masteries; no game of goblets, no morris-dance, might enliven their weary spirits, and the children which God vouchsafed them must be named by none other than a Bible name ! There's your boasted freedom ! "

When the Jesuit had concluded, Madame de Cornelli looked towards her daughter with a triumphant smile lighting up her eye, and seeming to say, " I knew he would prove it to our satisfaction." As for Marie, she rested her little chin thoughtfully on her hand, and became absorbed in her thoughts. At last she looked up, with a flush of anger mantling over brow and cheek, and said—

" I must crave your permission, your reverence, to except my father from the strictures which you have been applying to the Huguenots. I believe he follows an ideal as lofty and pure as man can set himself, and that if all Catholicism lay chained at his feet, he would stoop to unrivet the fetters and proclaim freedom of thought for all. You must pardon my speaking in an excited tone, father. I reverence the Church, but I will not stand by and hear my own beloved father dispraised."

" Sister, the heat with which you answer me does credit to your filial love. God pardon thee, if in aught thou hast preferred the natural yearning of the flesh to the spiritual things of God. True, most true, it is that monseigneur follows an ideal of his own, an ideal far above the sodden image of perfection set up by those with whom he consorts. There are men such as he, no doubt, in the ranks of the heretics, but they cannot leaven the whole lump; their society, my sisters, is a republic, where all are equal, where no gifts of intellect or piety avail to give one a commanding influence over the others, but where the noisy, fussy, third-rate intellect pushes its way to the front, and propels the society into a dangerous fanaticism."

As the Jesuit uttered the last words the door opened and three figures appeared—the sieur, followed by Philippe and Maintenon. All three had recently attended ·divine service in the temple, and all three paced sedately in the room with an air of gravity.

" Dangerous fanaticism ? " cried the sieur, catching up the last words ; " allow me to say, Monsieur le Jésuite, that it ill becomes you to make my lady's boudoir an arena for theological strife, and hard names are but ill arguments."

The arrival of the three heretics caused some commotion amongst the trio who had been so pleasantly discussing the affairs of the next

world.   Madame half rose with a flushed cheek,
and a shade of disquietude seemed to settle on
her brow, as she said—

"Mon cher, you mistake le bon cher père. It
is no theologic strife which has engaged us this
morning; indeed, had you overheard the whole
of the last sentence, you would have blushed
to hear yourself praised so well. If you *will*
know the subject of our talk—down, Maintenon! down, I tell you!—Father Beretti was
giving us some instances of intolerance among
your own elect, mon cher!"

The sieur kissed away the arch smile which
was hanging on his wife's lips as she pronounced these words, then extended his hand
to the Jesuit, as he replied—

"Thanks, good father, for your lessons from
history; but I trow you drew your examples of
intolerance from one side only. Ah! evil begets
evil, and it is somewhat difficult to turn one's
cheek to the smiter! I remember, when in 1663
I came away from seeing poor Morin, 'the Son
of Man,' as the lunatic styled himself, burnt at
the stake in Paris, I felt my bosom burning with
hellish fury against the cruel Church which could
so persecute a harmless fool. And when again,
father, you shut up Saci, the director of the

Port Royal nuns, in your infernal Bastille, with all my theories about religious freedom, I was then for crushing Papists all the world over. Believe me, ladies, you can't tolerate a Church that won't tolerate you! Self-preservation is nature's first law; and when you have stories told you of Huguenots persecuting Papists, it is only fair to remember what the good fathers of your Church have wrought in the way of fire and sword. The sentiment of revenge which has prompted some of our reprisals I do not defend; it is, however, human. But when men argue, 'If I don't kill you, you will kill me,' the blame surely lies with the one who first appeals to force."

The Jesuit, while the sieur was speaking, had been making friendly overtures to Maintenon, who lay under the sofa, resting his great tawny head on his fore-paws; but to all the father's offers of peace and amity the dog was deaf, and continued steadily eyeing his reverence in a calm offensive manner, which delighted the heart of Marie. At length he found an opportunity to say—

"Monseigneur will pardon me when I say he has forgotten one great distinction between our treatment of heretics and their persecution of us. Holding, as we do, the doctrine that there is no salvation outside the Church, together with that other which affirms the infallibility of the Church's teaching, we can do no other but chastise away all heresy—we can no more tolerate it than you can an open sewer or a dangerous lunatic. But when Huguenots begin to use force, they contradict the first principles of their own creed, which makes every man his own pope, and conscience the sovereign interpreter of religious truth. We act on principle ; you on impulse."

The sieur looked towards Marie, who had been attentively following the discussion, and replied—

"What think you, ma mie, about a principle which leads you to slaughter thousands of honourable lives ? Contrast it, I beg, at your leisure, with the precepts of our gentle Lord and Saviour, and ask yourself whether the Christ of Galilee would, if He were amongst us now, give the same counsel which He offered His apostles—' He that takes the sword shall perish with the sword' ? To my mind, Sir Jesuit, the logical conclusion to which your premises lead you is one of the strongest proofs that your principles are false. My gorge rises and my heart revolts at the bloody scenes enacted by the Inquisition, and I can only say that if the God you worship approves of your torturing and thumb-screwing and burning alive, that is not the Holy and Merciful Being whom I serve."

Madame de Cornelli at this moment rose, and, signing to Marie to give her her arm, quitted the chamber.

"I fear we have disquieted madame," said the Jesuit.

At this moment the door opened, and a servant entered bearing a sealed letter, which he said a special courier had brought.

"Excuse me," said the sieur, taking the despatch and preparing to retire ; "I must leave the conduct of our argument to my son, now."

"Or to your dog, monseigneur," replied Beretti, as Maintenon took the chair vacated by his master.

Madame de Cornelli and Marie were hardly seated in the bay window of the little sitting-room which opened into the sieur's bedroom, when Cornelli himself appeared with the letter which he had just unsealed.

"How do you feel, my dear wife ? Strong enough to travel to Jersey ? Ah ! good and brave wife! you will need all your nerve, I fear, if what the writer of this saith be true. Listen to what our friend Jean de la Bruyère writeth: 'You ask me, mon ami, to come and see you. I would that were possible, but my journey to Paris is so near at hand that I must not think of it. I know not if you have heard the latest news from court, but I give it you, in case you should not be fore-warned: the king has revoked the Edict of Nantes, and dragoons are on their way to Rouen. What thou doest, do quickly. I will buy thy estates and hold them in pledge for thee and thine. See that some trusty *avocat* has the business in hand. Farewell!'—Our plans now must be hastened, or it will be too late. To-morrow night I propose that you set out. I shall go forward to the coast with Philippe when it grows dark to-night, to make sure that our vessel is in readiness. Pierre and Constant, and Durand with his wife and children, and of course Mademoiselle Ethel, will accompany you."

"Hélas, mon mari, I would it were well over!"

The sieur kissed his wife tenderly, looking wistfully into the pale face, with such pitiful thoughts of what might be, that he well-nigh wavered in his resolution of quitting home and fatherland for conscience' sake.

"Go, Marie, and seek thy brother, while I stay here and comfort thy mother."

And Marie went downstairs as one in a dream, stunned by the suddenness of the blow; for she had never left her home, and all she loved was associated with the grey towers and swaying cedars of the Château de l'Esprit. She found Phil alone in the red boudoir, threw herself on his neck, and burst into tears.

"Oh, Phil, we are going away, going to a foreign land, and poor mamma——!"

"I am right glad," said her brother fiercely; "better far is freedom with want than lordly riches with slavery!"

"You do not understand, mon frère, all the risks we run by attempting to fly."

"Don't I, though? Mais oui, Marie; voyez donc! If papa and I are caught we shall be sent to the galleys for life, and if you or mamma are caught you will enter a convent; and then what will Henri do?"

"Hush, Phil! que tu es méchant."

CHAPTER XII.

WHEN Henri Guillot returned to Avranches with his father, he found a letter from his brother, saying that he had sought service with the Prince of Orange, and entreating Henry to follow his example; that there was no promotion for any but good Catholics in the navy of Louis, that William of Orange would gladly accept the services of any French gentleman who offered him his sword, and that both glory and emolument were to be won by serving in a navy which was destined to carry the Reformed Faith from the Netherlands to Spain. The young lieutenant took counsel with his father, and at length the two resolved to escape by sea to Holland, as France was no place for those who refused to put their consciences out to nurse. Before Henri sailed, however, he wrote a letter to his little friend Philippe, enclosing the portrait of his mother which, as we have seen, the boy presented to his sister in the cathedral at Coutances. No jewel could have expressed his feelings so pathetically as this valued relic, and Marie knew, when she received it, that she was accepting a pledge which he would one day come to her to redeem.

So inconsistent is woman, who even while she refuses a man's hand to-day, is terribly annoyed if he comes not to-morrow to solicit her anew! And Marie, having satisfied conscience by one energetic act of repulse, thought it proper to treat resolution by indulging in romantic dreams of what might yet come to pass. But the months passed, and no other letter came; and when, after waiting a long time in suspense, Marie at last ventured to ask her father if Captain Guillot was still in Avranches, she was startled to hear from him that the old man and the lieutenant had sailed for Holland. This was a sore trial of faith, and cost the young lady some tears; but when Ethel, who had been taken into confidence, suggested that the lieutenant might have taken this step from a desire to clear himself of the charge of atheism, hope put forth new buds, and fancy wove them into such a wreath as brides may wear.

For some months the Guillots remained at
Amsterdam, where they found quite a colony
of their own countrymen, haunting amongst
the gables of that Venice of the North, and
dangling their useless swords over the many-
bridged canals.

Captain Guillot procured an interview with
the Prince of Orange, and obtained commissions
for himself and his son in the Dutch navy; but
at present the service was merely nominal, and
many months of enforced idleness had to be
endured by the refugees.

To the old captain this retreat was welcome,
for there was no lack of old friends with whom
he would sit in some *cabaret* discussing the
chances of Louis and William, or playing
dominos with a good glass of Hollands by his
elbow; but the lieutenant found the time weary,
and voted the refugees a bore. He was tired of
listening to their tales of hair-breadth escapes,
and admiring the dancing of their poodles; and
as for the philosophers, Henri had no sympathy
with them, though he read their writings, and
went, with a young man's enthusiasm, as far
in the direction of free-thinking as the most
extreme. There was something of conceit, however, in all this; he would frequently return to

his chamber after disputing against the dogmas of Christianity, and kneel by his narrow bed to breathe a prayer in the name of Him whom he had recently all but denied. And at such times the thought of the mother at whose knee he learnt his first prayer would mingle with his devotions, and Marie's sad face, as it impressed itself upon him in the ball-room, would float before his eyes, till the hard-featured philosophy which had begun to shape his thoughts was ever and again melted and fused into the softer lines of religious sympathy. So impossible is it to love any human being devotedly without at the same time being drawn to love his God.

After lingering more than a year at Amsterdam, Henri removed to the Hague, in the hope of getting some post or mission, or of falling in some way under the notice of the Prince; but the number of needy Frenchmen who had flocked thither soon showed him that it was hopeless to seek advancement in that quarter. There was a truce, also, at this time between the French and the Dutch, and, though the latter were apparently increasing their navy, no great war was looming on the horizon. Henri would sometimes ride down to the shore, and taking a boat, pull about amongst the craft that lay at anchor there.

One evening in the spring of 1685 he was returning home on horseback along the straight avenue leading from the sea to the Hague, when in front of him he espied under the trees a man dismounted and struggling with his horse. As he drew near he noticed the long leather boots and sword of a cavalry officer, who was vainly trying to mount his steed; for, whenever the rider lifted foot to stirrup, round went the brute with a vicious kick, and a shake of the head which tasked the strength of his bridle.

"Can I be of any service to you, monsieur?" asked Henri, drawing rein.

"You can, monsieur. Have the goodness to draw alongside and seize my beast by the head. There! softly! enfin, j'y suis. I dropped my whip," he continued, on regaining his seat, "and getting down to pick it up, was unable to mount, as you saw. And now, monsieur, how can I return your kind assistance?"

Henri thought he detected rather a patronizing tone in the voice, and replied, with something of irony—

"By giving me a mount, monsieur, for I see you are of the court."

"Give you a mount? You speak in riddles, my friend."

"Make interest with your Prince to give me a ship, then. I long to be on the high seas, and I weary of this phlegmatic Dutchman."

"What! do you wish me to counsel my Prince—that phlegmatic Dutchman to whom you owe your asylum—to break the truce and rush into war to please a set of idle refugees?"

Henri touched the hilt of his sword instinctively, but replied—

"Oui, monsieur; you are in the right. I offended first; but at least I was not personal, and you were, for I am a refugee."

"And I am William of Orange," said the rider calmly.

For some seconds Henri could not answer, he was so astonished. At length he so far remembered himself as to take off his hat and apologize for his rude remark. The Prince of Orange laughed and bade him cover.

The two rode on together in silence.

"And what would you do if I gave you a ship?" said the Prince.

"Monseigneur, I would do the duty of a Protestant Prince, now generally looked upon as the protector of the Reformed Faith in

Europe. I would coast about and pick up the victims of priestly cruelty, opening fire on none save in self-protection."

"You can scarcely expect a phlegmatic Prince to approve so hazardous a course as that, monsieur?"

"Monseigneur has accidentally heard what I thought of his Highness. He will best refute me by granting my request."

"A pertinacious beggar, this Frenchman!" muttered the Prince.

The lights in the windows of the Stadt House were now appearing, and a group of gentleman had reined in their horses in the place beneath the chestnut-trees, who saluted William as he approached.

"We were beginning to be anxious, sire," said a veteran, whose hair was tinged with grey.

"Ah, Schomberg! After I sent you on, a slight accident detained me, which this gentleman kindly remedied. I pray you ask him his name and style, and bid him present himself to-morrow at eight of the clock. I would speak with him anon."

Accordingly Henri took leave of the Prince with a fluttering heart. Chance had done in a moment what the importunity of months had failed to effect. He retired to his lodgings to dream of naval battles and Marie offering wreaths of victory.

But William of Orange was not the man to offer a vessel, however small, to a chance comer. That night his secretary was examining into the antecedents of the sanguine young lieutenant; for in a neat, methodical register were inscribed, though they knew it not, the names, ages, quality, and past life of all the French refugees who had petitioned to serve under the Prince of Orange.

On the following day, then, Henri presented himself and found William attended by officers. Pointing to one who was in naval uniform the Prince said—

"This gentleman, Monsieur Guillot, is about to carry despatches to England, and has permission to do what he can for your countrymen. If you like to go on board, an officer unattached, you are welcome."

The lieutenant accepted the offer gratefully. Anything was better than the life of inactivity he had been forced to lead, and, after all, the despatch-boat might only be the excuse for an enterprise somewhat hazardous.

The sloop set sail for the mouth of the
Thames, and having left his despatches, the
captain made for the coast of France, where
they cruised about, picking up from time to
time fugitive Huguenots who had put out to
sea in open boats. When these grew too
numerous, the sloop returned and landed them
on the coast of Holland. It was on the third
of these cruises that Henri had begged the
captain to hug the shore of Brittany, that he
might land near Avranches and gather news of
his friends.

It was in October of the year 1685 that
Henri landed in a small boat a few miles north
of St. Michel. There he learnt from a fisherman, a well-known elder of the Church, that the
Sieur de Cornelli was in quest of a vessel to
transport his family to England. Henri therefore bade the fisherman hasten to the Château
de l'Esprit and acquaint the sieur with the fact
that a Dutch sloop was standing out in the
offing, and would await his orders, if he could
arrange the time and place with the messenger.

Now when the sieur set off with Philippe on
the Sunday night to arrange with Pierre Bart,
the fisherman, for a boat to convey his family
to the sloop, he was quite unaware that it was

Henri Guillot to whom he was indebted. His plan was to ride forward with Philippe and a groom to the point of embarkation, that he might be sure the vessel was one capable of carrying his party, then to return part of the way to meet the rest on the morrow. In case of accidents Pierre had stuffed two pistols in the holster, adding piously, as he pushed each home, " God bless thee ! "

As the father and son left their home the moon came out from a bank of clouds and lit up the château they were leaving behind, so that its long terraced walks and tapering turrets gleamed white between the moving trees, and the wind from the sea rustling amongst the yellow leaves seemed to whisper a hushed adieu ! The boy, thinking little of the past, and more of the adventure they were about to make, could not help breaking forth into a murmured song of gladness, as it were some bird fresh loosened from his cage. The father, whose thoughts were away with the happy days spent and gone, was plunged into a heavy sadness, which betrayed itself by deep sighs.

It is no light matter to give up a good estate and risk your liberty and the liberty of your wife and children—for what? For some speculative opinions on religion? Yet, after all, these same opinions, be they true or false in themselves, are worthy of being fought for, and are as precious to their owner as houses or lands; for he who fights for his opinions about God, does in fact fight for God, and he who surrenders them for the sake of gold or honour, does, in fact, sell his God for dross or the stinking breath of the multitude. Therefore let none sneer at the Huguenots who fled away from their country that they might worship the God they loved. With them it was no cowardice which prompted flight; rather were they the cowards who remained, saved their lands, and lost their peace of conscience.

After they had ridden on in silence for a mile or two, and were come to the brow of a hill whence they could see before them the sea and behind them the white glimmer of the château, the sieur pulled rein and paused to gaze upon the home of his ancestors, while a tear or two rolled unbidden down his cheeks.

"Oh, mon Dieu! am I justified in this?" he cried.

"Mon père," said Philippe, "the priests, not content with robbing you of your religious liberty, are trying all they can to rob you of wife and daughter. I overheard the Jesuit persuading mamma to quit you and enter a convent."

"Le scélérat! there is nothing these men will not do to compass their ends; as they phrase it, 'Dieu se sert de tous les moyens.'"

"Poor mamma! they have made her so miserable; n'est-ce-pas, mon père?"

"And yet, Phil, I am almost minded to turn back. What a horrible thing to expose you, mon cher, to a life in the galleys!"

"Ah, mon père, suffer me to strengthen you now, as you have so often strengthened me. Let us do what is right, in scorn of consequence. For my part, I fear not the galleys. God will find some means to help us; He will release us or give us strength to bear it, and besides, I do not fear we shall be stopped. The peasantry are all for us; no one will betray us to the guard which patrols the coast, and once on board, *vive la belle Angleterre!*"

The enthusiasm of the son communicated itself to the father, who lifted his head proudly and spurred his horse onward.

The moon had gone down, the night was dark, the wind moaned through the forest that lay on their left; they could hear the heavy roll of the breakers as they plunged sullenly on the shingly beach. A sudden turn in the road, and they rode down by the side of a brawling stream to the hospitable sea. There was a tiny red light twinkling hard by the cliff, and thither the travellers directed their course. The groom rapped at the frail. door with the butt end of his whip, and out came a drowsy fellow in a blue smock and long red cap which hung over one shoulder. He rubbed his eyes, muttered " Ventre-bleu ! I have slept!" helped Philippe to dismount with an " Entrez, monsieur," and a majestic air of welcome to which his limbs seemed to have been set, so mechanically precise were all his gestures, and taking up a lanthorn, showed the groom a shed where he could tie up the horses.

When the sieur entered the cabin he saw Philippe embracing some one with both arms and numerous kisses.

" Ah ! mon père, regardez donc ! See, it is our friend Henri !"

That night they fairly talked themselves to sleep in the fisherman's hut.

CHAPTER XIII.

Monday was a busy day at the château for those who were to make their pilgrimage to the coast in the evening. Mathilde, the old nurse, spent many an hour upstairs, collecting from a store of tiny garments, long disused, and strangely inappropriate to the wants of a sea voyage. Constant could not help drawing his cuff across his eyes as he relinquished his claim on perquisites too heavy to carry with him. Marie had flown to the white tower in the night to tell Ethel and the Durands to make ready for departure, and Pierre had summoned a synod of stalwart young heretics in the saddle-room, to whom he communicated the secret and a store of pikes and muskets. At one hour before midnight they were to assemble under the cedars as an escort to the ladies, who would ride securely in the great glass coach.

At noon the groom returned with a letter from the sieur, which was taken up by the old nurse to madame, who was reclining on her bed.

"Cheer up, my lady, v'là une lettre, voyez vous?" and the goody took from her mistress's hand the book of devotion in which she was forgetting her sorrow.

The letter was opened with a nervous tremor.

"Send Mademoiselle Marie to me, Mathilde."

When Marie came, her mother said, "Read your father's letter, ma chère, my eyes ache."

And Marie read :—

"MY DEAREST WIFE,

"All is well and in readiness for you all. The ship is a Dutch sloop, and who should be on board but Henri Guillot! He met me last night. It is a comfort to know we shall not be entirely amongst strangers. I shall meet you."

The mother and daughter exchanged looks.

"Marie, you knew nothing of Henri being there?"

Marie answered haughtily, "Ma foi, non!" And to tell the truth, she was glad to conceal her secret satisfaction under the veil of girlish indignation.

She wished she could have run to confide the wondrous news to Ethel, but her father had forbidden entrance to the white tower during daylight. So she carried the letter downstairs into the red boudoir, and read it over and over again; then, hearing steps in the outer hall, she quickly thrust it between some leaves of music which lay upon the table.

Immediately the door opened, and the footman ushered in Father Beretti. Alas! the window was open, too, and a gust of wind blew leaves and letter fluttering on to the floor. As the sieur's letter fell nearly under the sofa, Marie thought she heard a sigh come from it, and a shadow seemed to move and rest beside it. It was an evil omen.

She greeted the Jesuit with a dark look, and when he kissed her hand turned her head aside with an indifference almost akin to rudeness.

"I have come, my sister, to confer with your father, but they tell me he has gone to—to—Voyons! What was the name of the place?"

"My father has gone on business—*his own* business, your reverence."

"And when do you expect him back?" asked

the Jesuit, wincing slightly under the reproof of
the young lady's quiet sarcasm.

"We hope to see him to-night, but it is very
uncertain."

Baffled again, he asked no more questions.

"I hear the king has ordered twelve com-
panies of cuirassiers and twenty-four of the
royal étranger down to Rouen."

"We, too, have heard it. I believe they are
commanded by Choiseul-Beaupré," said Marie,
assuming an air of indifference.

"Monsieur le Marquis de Beuvron has orders
to assemble the chiefs of the pretended Reformed Faith in the Hôtel de Ville at Rouen.
They will have two hours given them to decide;
then, if they still refuse to abjure, the dragoons
will live upon them at free quarters."

"Mighty pleasant guests, your reverence!"
said Marie, with a laugh.

"Quoi! is it possible you do not think they
may come here also?"

"Why should they? We are Catholics here
—all but two."

"All but two, indeed! Methinks you speak
slightingly of your father."

Marie took no notice of the rebuke; an idea
occurred to her.

"O! perhaps you know where my father and brother are gone. Dites-moi donc, are they not gone to Rouen to abjure?"

The Jesuit elevated his eyebrows, and shrugged his shoulders.

"Non, ma sœur, you amuse me with your attempts to blind me. Monsieur votre père will never abjure; he is too proud for that!"

"And Monseigneur l'Évêque is far too charitable to allow the dragoons to trouble us; it would indeed be disgraceful, after all we have done for the Church."

"I know not," said the Jesuit, "what the bishop's personal feelings might be; but in these matters we must act for the good of all rather than for the interests of this man or that. 'Ad majorem Dei gloriam'—that is our watchword; with this thought our actions are instinct. Your father is a man of influence, and carries many along with him. Those who oppose the Holy Church must bend or break. I have come to-day to arrange for your good mother and you coming away. You will both be safer in a sisterhood for a time. And now, have the goodness to conduct me to your mother's room, that I may talk with her."

"My mother is not well, your reverence, and may not see you."

" If she is not well, all the more need for her confessor to visit her."

"Well, I will go and ask her permission," said Marie, rising to depart.

The Jesuit had risen to open the door, and on resuming his seat caught sight of the sieur's letter, which lay half-concealed under the sofa. It was of vital importance to the interests of the Holy Church that he should find out the whereabouts of the Sieur de Cornelli. It was repugnant to his feelings as a gentleman to be peeping into other people's letters, yet he could not help reading the first words, " My dearest wife, all is well and in readiness for you ;" and having read thus much he became all the more convinced that the best doctors of casuistry would pronounce this to be one of those cases where the " summum bonum omnium," or welfare of the whole, ought to be preferred to the secular pride of the individual. Accordingly, the good father stooped and put forth his hand to pick up the important missive, when an angry snarl made him start back and ejaculate, " Bon Dieu! it is that diabolical mastiff!"

Maintenon now had one paw firmly down on the paper, and his nose close to the floor, and to all the ecclesiastical soft-sawder which the

Jesuit tried upon him deigned to take no heed. However, it was important, in the interests of religion, that the father should read more, so he looked about for something with which he could draw the letter a little nearer to him. An old fiddle bow was lying in a corner, and with this he was proceeding, with words of blandishment, to filch the coveted paper from the dog's paw. A low growl warned him off, but either his strong sense of duty or his ignorance of canine fidelity prompted him to persist. No sooner had the fiddle-bow touched the letter than up sprang the dog with a furious howl, making the priest recoil against the table ; at the same time Maintenon sprang upon him with all his weight, snapping his great jaws close to the nose of the Jesuit, who, in his efforts to withdraw that organ out of harm's way, overturned the table, and himself with it, upon the polished oak floor.

The noise of the dog barking and the table falling summoned some of the servants, who, with Pierre at their head, rushed in to see what was the matter. Marie, too, came in, in time to see the father sprawling on his back, Maintenon standing over him with tail erect and bristling, her father's letter torn, half under the sofa, half lying by the table, and the fiddle-bow still grasped in the hand of the Jesuit, who seemed to have been stunned by the fall.

" Parbleu !" said old Pierre ; " his reverence has been playing out of tune, I doubt ; hé bien, an he be dead, Satan hath him afore he thought to. It's parlous work fiddling with an angry partner."

Marie stepped forward and picked up the letter, patted the dog on the head, who acknowledged the compliment by a backward motion of the ears.

" See, all of you," cried Marie, holding up the fragments ; " the priest has been trying to read my letter, and he has been foiled by that faithful hound."

Several voices muttered " Le maudit !" then two men picked up the Jesuit and carried him out into the hall, where Constant joined them. A short consultation was held, and then Pierre and Constant bore the unconscious confessor swiftly up the great staircase, and through the servants' lobby and the oaken door, into the colder atmosphere of the white tower, in the upper chamber of which they locked him up' and left him.

" He will do no harm there, at any rate,"

quoth Constant, "and can bide till the morrow, when we shall be safe on board, let us hope."

"And as yesterday was a feast in his church, 'tis only right to-day should be a fast," said Pierre, with a wink.

Marie returned to her mother, and found her pacing up and down the chamber, perturbed at the thought of confronting her confessor. She recounted what had happened in the boudoir, and how the Jesuit had been stunned by his fall and carried out by the servants. Madame de Cornelli was relieved when she found that her struggle to get free of priestly interference was postponed, though she was grieved that one she reverenced should have acted so basely. It was one more weight in the scale that was settling down towards husband and children and peace in a foreign land, and life in a French convent was continually growing less charming to her imagination.

"Ah, Marie!" she said, "if I can only take a good conscience with me, I shall not regret either the riches of this actual life in Normandy, or the riches of a possible spiritual life in some sweet sisterhood."

"Soyez contente, ma mère ; the good God has made you a mother, and no doubt He expects you to fulfil the duties He lays upon you. But rest awhile; I go to see if Mathilde has all things ready."

The day seemed to pass slowly to those inmates of the château who were to take part in the flight to the sea. They kept nervously flitting about the halls and passages, each bent on seeing if his neighbour had all things ready. Adolphe had already imbibed enough cider to render his tongue somewhat too voluble, when Constant laid an embargo on the distillery, and locked up the dangerous fluid.

By nine o'clock most of the servants had retired to bed, and the château seemed to have lapsed into profound silence; but some of the maid-servants, as they lay awake, thought they heard the cry of some one imprisoned in the white tower. They rose and alarmed their fellows, who all huddled together against the oaken door, shivering with superstitious fear, or applying their ear to catch some less uncertain sound. " It is the devil coming to damn the heretics," quoth one. " It is the unbaptized ghost of mademoiselle," quoth another. " It is the fiend of unbelief," cried a third; but whilst with bated breath they listened or whispered, a horrible sound of creaking locks smote upon their ears.

Yes; the mysterious door was turning on its hinges! They were riveted to the spot with terror, their limbs cold and clammy, their hair bristling, their knees smiting together. It seemed an hour before the door was open; they would have prayed, but the foul fiend had stolen away their memories.

" Ah, miséricorde !" they shrieked, as a white and hooded figure stood in the doorway, started back at the first sight of the cowering half-naked figures, then smiled a ghastly smile as she held up a lamp and closed the door behind her.

·" I am the ghost of Ethel Digby, and this is my private promenade! Away to your beds, or I shall carry you all to hell !"

At these words off they scampered right and left to their bedrooms, and as they ran seemed to hear the ringing laugh of the spirit as it paced along the sounding corridor.

Marie was already dressed for the journey when Ethel tapped at her door, and the two girls had a hearty laugh at the expense of their superstitious maidens.

" I have laid them for to-night, dear Marie; they will not dare to peer about now, lest I carry them off to the place of brimstone."

"It is very clever of you to think of such a trick; but how knew you that they were all standing without?"

"Ah! that's the strange thing which I cannot understand. You must know, Marie, that we were waiting, the Durands and I, for Pierre to summon us to the temple, when a terrific yelling and beseeching sounded over our heads. We were amazed and frightened, thinking the tower must be haunted, for we knew nobody was in it but ourselves. At last I plucked up courage to take the keys (for Constant had given me a duplicate) and come forth to ask you what it could mean, when lo! on opening the door, I saw a crowd of women with wild gestures and dishevelled hair. Oh! how weak I felt at that moment! But when I saw they shrank from me I bethought me of the stratagem I have just told you. But what, I prythee, could have been the clamour which so alarmed us in the tower?"

"Oh! *sans doute* 'twas Father Beretti," said Marie, laughing, and she proceeded to give her friend the narration of that gentleman's discomfiture and confinement.

At ten o'clock, under the pale moonlight, figures were moving across the lawn behind the château, and emerging from the shadows of the

apple-trees and rustling through the long grass.
By a small door, through which streamed a red
light, stood two men with lanthorns, and as
each person approached to enter the temple,
they raised the lights and scanned the face of
him who claimed admission.

Inside, a strange scene presented itself; flambeaux and torches lit up the chapel, which was
nearly filled with men and women and children
of all ages, the males standing on one side, the
females on the other. Most of the men were
covered, but a few had removed their hats. All
were talking in an excited manner; some were
embracing each other, as if for the last time,
with tears and sobs. So far had they gone in
divesting themselves of superstition, that they
had lost much of reverence for the house of
God. It is the penalty of all good revolutions,
excess on the other side; for even while some
layman was reading from the pulpit a chapter
out of the Bible, hats were worn and murmured
conversation kept up; but the form of respect
which is usually paid to the consecrated building
was not withheld from the pasteur, for as soon
as La Rose entered through the door communi-
cating with the château they all rose and
saluted him, "The Lord be with you!"

"And with you, my children!" answered the old man, bowing low on either side.

Then, as he mounted the stairs which deviously conducted to the pulpit, there was a great settling down into their benches, and throats were cleared, and much unconstrained spitting was rife for several minutes. Then the grey-haired pasteur took his hymn-book and gave out a psalm, and with one voice old and young, as they sat, sang from memory and in unison, slowly, but with feeling. When the last wail of the psalm had ceased to reverberate, all rose to their feet, and La Rose commenced a prayer. The old man was so affected as he asked a blessing on the house of the Cornelli that his voice broke more than once, and as he proceeded to recount the manly virtues of the sieur, and the present help in time of trouble which he had always been to Catholics and Reformed alike, a loud sob from the gallery made his hearers look up and see Madame de Cornelli on her knees, her head buried in her hands. Then the pasteur prayed for her who was with them, though not of them, and invoked the divine protection on her who had so often protected the poor and the oppressed. And in the pause which ensued there was audible the sound of childish weeping in the gallery, and those who looked up saw little Jeannette put her frail arms about the lady's neck and whisper. And when all was over and the faithful had dispersed, save two or three who still lingered about the door, one came up to Pierre, saying—

"Surely God will be gracious to the poor lady and her family, and get them safe across the sea!"

The old *serviteur* slowly shook his head as he replied—

"Nay, brother, I misdoubt it much, since that little wench that they call Jeannette invoked the Scarlet Woman."

"Bon Dieu, camarade! what was it the little jade said?"

"Why, she put her arms about madame's neck, and said—aye, she positively dared to say it in the temple, when Monsieur la Rose was praying so fine——"

"Hé! quoi, camarade! and what did the little vixen say, then?"

"Why, she hoped the Virgin Mary would come with us, too!"

"C'est impossible!"

"Si! I heard with these very ears, and I wonder I wasn't struck dead, I do."

"And what did madame say?"

"Ventre-bleu! I couldn't hear; but she hugged the little mischievous creature to herself, and it's my belief she's an imp of darkness!"

"Who? who? vite, camarade!"

"Why, the wench; the master stonemason has gone and begot the devil incarnate! And I am afraid to travel with her—only I carry a pistol and a silver bullet;" and the old coachman tipped his co-religionist a wink which was intended to escape the notice of the satanic authorities.

By eleven o'clock Madame de Cornelli and Marie and Ethel had mounted into the glass coach, which had been drawn up at some distance from the château, to avoid awaking those left behind; the page Adolphe and old Mathilde sat behind, Pierre and Constant were on the box, and another carriage followed carrying the Durands and some *serviteurs* of "the Religion." Besides these, some young farmers rode by the side of the coach, armed with the old-fashioned flint musket or arquebus.

At the lodge gate there was an affecting parting between Pierre and his mother. The old Ribston-pippin had stoutly refused to leave her home, and as the coach drove through she launched a few texts of warning import at the head of her audacious son.

"The Lord bless you, mother!" cried Pierre, waving his hand.

"I would cry the same on you, mon Pierre, but I can't expect it on Him; I solidly can't . . ." The rest of her objurgation was swept away by the west wind, which blew salt from the gulf.

"Three hours and we are free!" shouted Adolphe.

"Hush, you fool!" whispered Mathilde; "hush! you will raise the patrol!"

END OF VOL. I.